Bridesmaids' Club

Cathy Hopkins

MACMILLAN CHILDREN'S BOOKS

Chapter One

The Bridesmaids' Club

'Hey, Chloe, when do you think you'll hear from Marcie?' asked Demi as she cut out some pages from the February issue of *Weddings*.

'Any day now,' I replied as I looked at the magazine over her shoulder. 'I can't wait.'

It was our monthly get-together of the Bridesmaids' Club and it was just the three of us there. Me and my mates Demi and Maryam. We always made it to the meeting, first Saturday morning of every month, held at one of our houses. We saw each other for loads of other things outside the club because we're best friends but our Bridesmaids' Club was a non-negotiable event – like Christmas Day or Easter, it was part of our calendar. We had started it back when we were nine when we went to a wedding show in a nearby village called Osbury for a laugh. We had such a top time trying all the samples and living the bridesmaids' dream that we decided we wouldn't leave it there. We'd start a club and talk dresses, accessories, honeymoon locations and all the rest every month. In the meantime, we'd put together files to be used by friends who needed wedding advice. We'd made ourselves experts. Other girls came and went as their various relatives got married but us three, we were regulars, rain or shine, wedding or no wedding.

My mum teased me that the club was my religion but then my whole family teased me about everything, me being the youngest and more romantic and into girlie stuff than any of my three career-driven older sisters. Maybe I'm into it all because of my star sign – not that I particularly believe in astrology and all that stuff but I did read somewhere that Libras are known for their love of beauty. That's me. I do like nice things, always have, and everything to do with weddings is fairy-tale lovely.

'I wonder how he'll do it,' said Maryam. 'Is he the down-on-one-knee type?'

She was talking about my sister Marcie's boyfriend, Geoff. Marcie had been dating him for about six months. He'd swept her off her feet in a whirlwind romance after she'd split up with a guy who had broken her heart. When Geoff booked a long weekend in Paris, we all suspected that this was it. Proposal time.

I shrugged in answer to Maryam's question. 'I hope

so. Marcie likes a bit of romance when the mood takes her.'

Demi and Maryam nodded. Marcie was an honorary member of the Bridesmaids' club and secretly loved all that romantic stuff. She was my favourite sister, the best in the world – even though she didn't live at home any more, she was round a lot and always had time for me. The only blip had been when she was dating Sam. I was so relieved that she broke things off with him and met Geoff. Sam used to tease me about the Bridesmaids' Club, which he thought was a joke.

My other two sisters, Jane and Clare, think I'm too immature to waste their days off on so I was thankful that I had at least one sister who was occasionally up for shopping trips and could be persuaded into sessions of DIY pampering, painting nails and trying out face packs. Marcie was great. She'd always been there to drive me and my mates to the cinema, to play practical jokes on us, to see the latest chick flick, then laugh, gossip and eat chips from the paper on the way home. And I'd seen her watch romantic movies and blub even though she'd try to hide it. Until, that is, what I call her lost period, when she was with the thunder from down under, Mr Sam Lycra Shorts Hendy (he was from Australia). She totally changed when she was with him and it was bye-bye Marcie, hello Lara Croft, action girl. With Sam, she'd been white-water rafting, camping under the stars, climbing mountains. My Marcie who didn't even own a pair of trainers pre Sam – who only did five-star luxury hotels on holidays and thought sleeping in tents was for losers! I was so with her on that – not that I'd stayed in many five-star hotels, but I knew that when I was older I would rather sleep in the softest linen and have a bathroom with fluffy white towels than doss out in a damp sleeping bag in a tent and have to go to the loo in some stinky bucket. All part of being Libran apparently. We don't like to rough it. Anyway, Marcie's back to normal, thanks to Geoff.

She never owned up to Sam about being a member of the Bridesmaids' Club because of his views about weddings. He thought that marriage and all that went with it was a waste of time. Marcie didn't tell Clare and Jane either, because she didn't want to be seen as an airhead who was easily carried away by a bit of sparkle. As if. She's got a degree in quantum physics. Our whole family are brainboxes, me included. I am always top of our year in most subjects. Dad is a scientist (he doesn't live with us any more – he and Mum are divorced and he lives with his new wife in Wales), Mum and Clare are lawyers and Jane lectures at the local university – her subject is statistics. Like, how dull is that?

Clare and Jane had both done me out of my chance to be a bridesmaid. 'No time to waste on men,' said Clare soon after she left home. 'I don't need anyone to share my life with. I am perfectly happy on my own. My career is what matters.' She does date men occasionally, usually through the Internet, but they never last. I think she eats them for breakfast or buries them under her patio – she sees men as disposable and not completely necessary. Jane does have a steady boyfriend and after they had been together a few years, I thought maybe I'd get my chance to be bridesmaid. But no, she announced that they don't need a piece of paper to show that they are serious, so they live together as 'partners'. I did everything I could to talk her into getting married, but she cut me off, saying that the West was steeped in materialism and that marriage was just another consumerist event to rob decent people of their money by feeding them an unrealistic fantasy. Like, *whoa*, OK, so that might be true but I can see the other side. The fun side. Needless to say, Sam got on well with Jane and Clare, because they all shared the same views about marriage.

At one time, I had hoped that Mum might remarry but she swears that she never will. She says that men let you down. I think my dad leaving hurt her and my sisters more than they let on. He left when I was still a baby so I don't miss him because I don't remember him. All I know is that, because of him, my mum and sisters are suspicious of men.

It's so not fair. Demi and Maryam have both had goes at being bridesmaids. Demi *twice*, once with her sister, Rose and once with her auntie Mags. But soon, very soon, it might be my turn and it'll be utterly FAB-ulous. Demi's aunt had been a winter bride and her sister a spring, and Maryam had been an autumn bridesmaid so I wouldn't want to replicate. Not that I wasn't prepared, if Marcie and Geoff chose winter for the big day – the wedding could be held in a castle in the Scottish Highlands or maybe Ireland. I could just see it. It would be snowing. Marcie would sweep up in a horse-drawn sleigh. She would be wearing ankle-length white velvet with a long cloak, a crown of ivy on top of her flowing hair. Very medieval princess. If it was to be summer, we could jet off to some fabulous island: the Caribbean, the Seychelles or the Maldives. Yeah. We'd be jet-set cool. I had all the maps and stacks of brochures showing couples kissing in the surf at sunset. Marcie could wear a shimmer of ivory silk, cut on the bias, possibly backless to show off her per-fect even tan, her hair caught up at the back in a sophisticated style dotted through with tiny pearls and flowers. Or if they didn't want to travel far, we could book some gorgeous hotel in the country, very English, Marcie in an off-the-shoulder sheath dress. She'd look fab. I'd look fab. Whatever the season or location, I would follow her wearing something stunningly original. *Not* lilac. Or candy pink. Or anything with mutton sleeves. Or bows. The guests would gasp. A wall of cameras would click. We'd feature in all the glossies where page after page would gush on about how we made the most *gorgeous* wedding party ever seen. And they'd be right too. Marcie scrubs up well when she can be bothered to make the effort and I am five foot four, have long legs, 32A chest, shoulder-length blonde hair. Perfect bridesmaid material.

Geoff never once laughed or teased me when he found out about the Bridesmaids' Club. He was genuinely interested when he heard about it and asked how it got started and what we did and so on. I really do intend to make Marcie's wedding the best ever. *Ever.* Not that Demi and Maryam aren't pretty. They are. Maryam is dark-skinned with gorgeous black curls to her shoulders and the most amazing huge brown eyes. She looked like a Caribbean princess in an ivory dress when her sister got married. Demi is pale and tall with long dark hair. Her sister did the pink thing for her bridesmaids and Demi made it work by having an all-over spray tan the day before so that she didn't look washed out (pale pink can be a hard colour to wear unless you're a blonde like me).

Loads of our mates at school, who were drop-in members of the Bridesmaids' Club, had already had their big days too. Susie Jenson had been bridesmaid last spring – a wedding held in a posh country hotel. She was passing round the photos for weeks afterwards. I ooh-ed and aah-ed as you do, but I was thinking, *Just wait until it's my turn. Then you'll see something really special.* And then it was Tara Peters' go. A rhapsody in shocking pink. Talk about Tack City! There are shades of pink and some of them just don't work for a wedding. Jess Lewis was next: cream with too many ribbons and bows, for a shepherdess kind of look. Bows? Double yuck.

I can't wait to hear what Marcie and Geoff want. Not that it will be a problem whatever they choose. There isn't an aspect or an area of weddings that I don't know about. I've been collecting ideas for years, ready for my turn – and now it may be about to happen. I couldn't wait. My bridesmaid album was bursting at the seams. I added to it all the time – I cut dresses out of *Brides* magazine or anything else that took my fancy in the glossies. I had fabrics, dresses, jewellery, shoes, hairstyles, veils, locations for the ceremony and locations for honeymoons – every aspect of weddings there was. Best of all, Marcie had always been open to all my suggestions, whether it be for table arrangements, flowers for the church, register office or a posh country mansion. I had vintage cars, limos, American cars, open carriages, snow sledges . . . you name it, lined up. Marcie was happy to leave it all to me. All that had been missing was the groom and that I couldn't help her with.

For a short time when she was single after Sam, she was so heartbroken that she said she would never date again, and I was just beginning to wonder if she was doomed to be on her own forever when along came Geoff. Tall, dark and handsome, a friend of hers introduced them at a dinner party and there was no going back. I was so relieved. Sam had been wrong for Marcie and not only because of his love of sport and adventure holidays but also because he was commitment shy (which was the real reason they broke up) and according to Marcie, rubbish at communicating his feelings. Even though Marcie went along with the rugby, hiking, surfing, tennis and climbing, I reckoned she wouldn't have been able to keep it up for a lifetime.

But Geoff fits the role of handsome prince perfectly and Marcie said he's very happy to talk about feelings. Plus he always lets her have her own way and make all the decisions about how they are going to spend their time. When the Paris trip was announced a few weeks ago, I felt that my life's ambition was about to be achieved and the fairy-tale wedding was set to rock and roll.

Demi clicked her fingers in front of me. 'Hey, dreamer! Earth to planet Chloe,' she said. 'We were supposed to be thinking about what we want to do when we leave school. Our weekend's homework, remember? Have you decided?'

They both looked at me for my answer. I put my hands up as if to say I didn't know. Indecision is one of my biggest problems. Always has been (another Libran trait according to my *Girl in the City* magazine's astrology page). I never know what I want outside of being in the Bridesmaids' Club. 'Still not sure. I can't decide. It's OK for you guys – Maryam, you've wanted to be a fashion designer since the moment you were born, and, Demi, you've got your photography.'

Maryam nodded. 'Never changed for me. But what about you? You must have some idea.'

'Nope. Don't know. Mum thinks that I'd be a good lawyer because I'm good at seeing both sides of an argument but I think, lawyer? Boring. And course Dad wrote to me and advised me to follow in his footsteps and do science but no way do I want to be stuck in a laboratory all my life and why should I listen to him? He never comes to visit and he's not really part of my life so why should he get a say? I wish everyone would get off my case. Like, I'm fourteen – it's ages until we have to choose our subjects.'

'No it isn't,' said Demi. 'Mr Mooney said we have to decide in the next few weeks.'

'Then I'll say I want to be a road sweeper and study collecting rubbish,' I said. Neither of them laughed. 'Oh, come on guys, chill out. I have enough with Mum, Dad and three sisters going on at me about what I should do and how hard I have to study to get there without you two doing it as well.'

At that moment, from the back pocket of my jeans, my phone bleeped that I had a text. I pulled it out and glanced at the screen. Demi and Maryam looked at me expectantly.

I nodded. 'Marcie.'

Chapter Two

Wedding Show

'OK,' said Demi as we took in the hundreds of stands in the vast tent that had been decorated from corner to corner with pink sparkly banners and hundreds of heart shaped-balloons. 'Let's start at the left and go up one aisle, down the next and so on so that we don't miss anything.'

Maryam and I gave her a salute. 'Right,' I said. It was a week after Marcie had announced her engagement and we were at the annual wedding show on the green in Osbury. Marcie had sounded very happy when I spoke to her. I wanted all the details but she said that her phone card was running low, so although she could confirm that she was definitely engaged to be married and that they wanted to do it in June, she'd fill me in on the rest later. I was dying to know how he'd proposed. She promised she'd tell me everything when she came home next and I could hardly wait.

In the meantime, there was the wedding show. It was held every year around Valentine's Day and already I could see some familiar faces. A pretty brunette at a jewellery stall waved so we trooped over.

'Hi, Chantelle,' we chorused.

'Hey, girls,' she said. 'You here again?'

'Wouldn't miss it,' said Demi.

'And this year, *I* have a wedding to plan,' I said. 'A very special wedding.'

'Who?' asked Chantelle.

'My sister Marcie,' I replied. 'Her boyfriend took her to Paris to propose.'

Chantelle sighed. '*How* romantic. I'd *love* to be taken to Paris.'

'I know. Me too. I'm going to make her relive every detail when she gets back.'

Chantelle laughed. 'So what kind of wedding does she want?'

'Not sure yet. She's still away but she's coming over next weekend for Sunday lunch and we'll discuss it then.'

'We're here to get ideas,' said Demi.

'Get the ball rolling,' said Maryam.

'The show's such perfect timing,' I said.

'She's a lucky girl, is your sister,' said Chantelle, 'having you lot to do her research. You be sure and tell her about my range, won't you? Though I suppose if he's already asked her to marry him then she's got the ring?'

13

I nodded. 'I guess, though I haven't seen it yet.'

'I'd better get on, girls,' said Chantelle when a customer began looking at her stall. 'Enjoy the show and check out Aisle H. There are some new people down there. Call themselves Celestial Weddings. I haven't seen any of them before and they look like a fun bunch.'

'Aisle H. Will do,' I said.

We set off to roam the stalls and soon we were caught up in the usual show frenzy as traders thrust brochures and leaflets at us and various salespeople beckoned us to come and sample what was on their stall.

'You're so lucky to have a wedding this year,' said Demi as she looked through an album on one stall showing floral arrangements for the ceremony.

'I know,' I said and I gave myself a hug. 'I've been waiting *all* my life for this.' I loved the annual wedding show. I loved it even more than Christmas and birthdays, more than Easter with all the chocolate. I loved the glamour, how pretty everything was. I loved the dream. It was true, everything my sisters said about the wedding industry selling a fantasy, but that was exactly what I *liked* – that for one day, someone could be transported into another world – an enchanted world where the bride was a princess and the groom was her prince. A world where everyone looked their most beautiful and happy, where people danced merrily, butterflies flitted, doves cooed, where there was music and flowers and delicious food, a yummy scrummy cake and a celebration of love. So my family dissed it. In my opinion, they were *seriously* missing out on one of life's true joys.

We cruised the stalls for an hour or so, tried every freebie, greeted old friends: Jason on honeymoon destinations, Elena on Belgian chocolates, Moira on Tux and Tails, Arthur on wedding invites, Georgina on dresses for the mothers-in law, Anna Lee on shoes. We chomped on samples of wedding cake, ooh-ed and aah-ed over the dresses modelled in a fashion show, sat in a white wedding limo and sipped on sparkling apple juice. We entered every competition that was going. It was part of the fun. There were prizes from the cheap to the spectacular, for make-up, makeovers, jewellery, cakes, cars, a weekend in the Caribbean for a lucky bride and groom – you name it. The fair organizers always announced the winners up on the stage at the end of the show and made a big fuss over them. So far, none of us had won anything but that didn't stop us from entering every year. We tried on a variety of tiaras and turned our noses up at anything we thought looked cheap or tacky.

'*So* downmarket,' said Demi with a disapproving sniff as we surveyed one stall that sparkled with eye-dazzling bling. I nodded in agreement with her but I didn't even mind the tack. I felt so happy. This was my world. I loved every minute of it and could never understand why everyone else didn't feel the same.

Next was a stall with men's aftershaves and we had a sniff of a few. Some smelt too strong, like pot pourri with a slice of lemon. Yuck! I prefer the subtler scents, the classics, like Chanel or Armani. I remembered that Marcie had said that Sam smelt like the sea – sand dunes and salty air. She said that it was one of the things she liked so much about him – his natural scent. Pff! That wouldn't have been right for a wedding. Eau de Sand Dune. I am sure that Geoff will wear Armani on the day if we tell him to because he does everything Marcie asks.

'So what do you think so far?' asked Demi when we reached Aisle H, where I could see that Chantelle had been right, there did appear to be some new faces.

'Hmm,' I said. 'I've seen a few things I think Marcie might like. I think that as she's getting married in June, we should go for the classic summer look. An ivory sheath of silk. Marcie's got the perfect slim figure for that kind of dress.'

Demi sighed. 'She's going to look so beautiful.'

'I know,' I agreed. *And so am I*, I thought. I'd seen a number of bridesmaids' dresses that would look great on me. It depended on what colours Marcie wanted and if she wanted just me as her bridesmaid or if she wanted Demi and Maryam too. It was going to be fun deciding everything. Usually having to make choices is my worst nightmare because I can never make up my mind but when it came to planning a wedding, the millions of choices to make made it all the more enjoyable.

We began to walk down Aisle H, where there were a few new stalls to look at, all with the same logo on a banner behind the stall. It said 'Celestial Weddings' and had stars and planets whizzing around the words. *That sounds good*, I thought as we took a closer look. One stall had samples of wedding invites, all tasteful and elegant. For future reference, I made a note of the name of the designer on the back: Hermie at Mercury Communications, part of Celestial Weddings. Another stall had a fabulous array of wedding foods, behind which was a jolly-looking man, who introduced himself as Joe Jupiter, then offered us a sample of cake. I took a piece and bit into it. It was light and melted in your mouth with a burst of white chocolate

'Wow!' I said. 'This is divine.'

He beamed back at me and gave me his card. 'Europa Catering for Celestial Weddings', it said, 'Food Fit for the Gods'.

Demi stopped at a stall that appeared to have no one manning it. 'Be a goddess for a day,' said a poster underneath the logo behind the stall. On the table at the front there was a large white book with silver edging. I flicked it open to see a portfolio of dresses.

'Fabulous,' said Maryam as I looked at the first. It was my favourite kind of wedding dress – a simple sheath cut on the bias, elegant and classic.

'And that model is stunning,' said Demi.

I took a closer look. Demi was right. The model was amazing looking. 'Wow! She's a good advertisement, isn't she? She actually *looks* like a goddess.' We turned page after page of the most fabulous dresses, all modelled by the same woman. Each dress was beautifully cut with extras of lace and mother-of-pearl sewn in here and there, just enough to make them different from others on show but not so much that they stood out as over the top.

'She's not a model I've ever seen before,' said Maryam. 'Maybe she's new to the business?'

I looked on the book for her name. 'Designs by Nessa and modelled by Nessa', it said at the bottom of the page. How cool, one name – like she didn't need a surname.

'These are the best designs I have *ever* seen in all our years of coming to the show,' I said as I looked around. 'So graceful.'

Demi and Maryam nodded in agreement. 'And look,' said Demi as she picked up a leaflet from the table, 'she does makeovers too. "Hair and make-up by Nessa."'

'I wonder who she is and if she's here at the show,' I said.

Maryam suddenly tugged on my arm. 'Hey, look at this,' she said and she pulled me towards the next stall.

'Horoscopes!' said Demi and she began to read the board at the right of the table. '"Plan your perfect day by the stars."'

'Wow, astrology! I've never seen a stall advertising that here before, have you—'

'I know. I'm the first. Ridiculous, isn't it?' said a male voice.

We turned to see a tall slim man standing to our right. He was dressed in a white sparkly jumpsuit with his silver-white hair spiked up, and was beautiful in an elfin prince kind of way. He looked like he belonged in a sci-fi or fantasy film. He certainly didn't look like any of the other stallholders, who were dressed in trad- itional wedding outfits or in ordinary clothes. This man looked like he'd landed from a distant planet.

'I'd say that it's very important to make sure that you're getting married on a day when the stars are lined up favourably, wouldn't you?' he continued.

'Yes. Course. Yes,' I said. 'I'd never thought of that.' I didn't know a lot about astrology apart from a few things about Librans but I did know that some days were supposed to be good and some not so good according to where the Sun or Moon was.

'I mean, can you imagine if you'd set the day and say Saturn and Mars were square to each other or even worse, Saturn and Venus in opposition – that might be a disaster. Venus is the planet of love and harmony, you know. It's very important that's in the right place on someone's special day.'

I felt slightly in awe of him, but had to agree he was talking sense. I had read once in Mum's newspaper that one of the Presidents of America consulted an astrologer regularly and if *he* had done it over important things like running a country then it was probably a good idea to consult one over planning a wedding.

'How can we get a horoscope done?' I asked.

'Here,' said the man. 'My name's Uri and I can do it for you.' He indicated a computer on the stall. 'All I need from you is the date and place and time of birth of the bride and groom.'

'The bride's my sister. I know she was born on August 9th, not far from here, but I don't know what time and I don't know the wedding date yet – she only just got engaged and they haven't set the day yet although I think it will be June. And um, Geoff's birthday is . . . let me think, November 30th . . . oh no, that's Sam's, um, he was her ex. Geoff . . . Geoff's birthday? March. Yeah. March 7th, that's it, and he was born in Bristol and lived there all of his life with his mum until she died last year.'

Demi sighed. 'Lucky he met Marcie so soon after, poor thing,' she said.

'Yeah. He might have been really lonely otherwise,' I agreed.

Uri beamed. 'OK. So the bride is a Leo. They are compatible with other fire signs usually – Aries and Sagittarius. Did you say that the groom's birthday was November 30th? That's good. That would make him a Sagittarius. Leos and Sagittarians are a *great* match.'

'No. No. November was Sam's birthday. Geoff is March 7th.'

Uri frowned. 'He'll be a Pisces then.'

'Is that a good match?' asked Demi.

'Um . . . I need the exact time to do it properly.'

'Why?' asked Demi.

'You can only find out what your sun sign is from your date of birth. You see, your sun sign changes every month, but your moon sign changes every two days and your rising sign changes every two hours. All the different factors are what make each chart totally unique.'

'Whoa! Information overload. Sun sign? Moon sign? Rising sign? I thought there were only twelve signs of the Zodiac,' said Demi.

'True,' said Uri. 'Aries, Taurus, Gemini, Cancer,

Leo, Virgo, Libra, Scorpio, Sagittarius, Capricorn, Aquarius and Pisces. But that's only the tip of the iceberg. They all have ten planets that affect them, not just the sun – if that was all there was to it, everyone born under the sign of Capricorn would be exactly the same, wouldn't they? Astrology is more of a science, which is why I need date of birth, time and place. The place is important because someone born in Scotland and another born in America at the same time on the same day will also have different characteristics because the stars will all be at different angles to the earth. Right?'

'I guess,' said Demi. 'I never thought of that.'

'Can you do our horoscopes too?' asked Maryam.

Uri nodded. 'Sure,' he said. He looked at me. 'You're a Libran, yes?'

I nodded.

'Do you know much about your sign?' he asked.

'A bit,' I replied. 'Like we're supposed to be romantic and like beautiful things.'

Uri nodded. 'Indeed. Librans are a nice sign. Charming is another trait.'

I gave him what I hoped was my most winning smile and he laughed.

'Charming, easy-going, sociable, lovers of beauty,' he continued. 'They love to dress up, like the good things in life, and have a great eye for quality and true style.' I curtseyed to the others. It felt good having such complimentary things said about me. 'On the other hand, every sign has a dark side and for Librans, it's that they can be indecisive and changeable.'

'That's true,' I said. 'I can never make up my mind about *anything*.'

'They can also be easily influenced, they don't like being rushed, they can be self-indulgent, shallow—'

'Hey,' I said. 'Shallow?'

'Shallow and self-indulgent,' he said.

'That's not very kind,' I said.

'And they don't like to be criticized either,' said Uri. 'Oh no. They can be bossy too as they like their own way.'

Demi and Maryam giggled and nodded.

'Generally, they are a lovely sign though,' said Uri. 'Easy-going and good company.'

'Huh!' I said. I wasn't sure what to make of it. I certainly wasn't feeling very easy-going after having been told that I was shallow and self-indulgent. Luckily Uri shifted his focus and looked at Demi. 'Gemini?' She nodded. He looked at Maryam. 'Sagittarius.' She nodded. While they chatted to Uri, I got out my mobile and tried Marcie's number. It went straight on to voice mail. 'I'll call home,' I said. 'Mum'll think I'm barmy though. In fact, all my family would laugh if they knew I was doing horoscopes.'

The three of us found a quiet spot in the tent and each of us phoned home. As I had expected, Mum gave me the usual inquisition. 'Why do you need your time of birth? You're not to give personal details to a stranger because they could be used for identity fraud.'

'Oh Mum, I know that. But even if someone did steal my identity, what are they going to steal from me? I haven't exactly got millions in a bank.'

'Then tell me what it's for.'

'I want to get my horoscope done—'

'Horoscope! That nonsense. Oh, for heaven's sake, Chloe.'

'It's not nonsense. Actually, if you gave it a chance, you'd realize that it's, um . . . scientific. And I want to do Marcie's too. Oh, come on, Mum, let me have the time of birth. Uri can't do it without.'

'Uri. Uri! Who's Uri?'

'He's the astrologer.'

'Good Lord, Chloe. Where are you?'

'The wedding show. I told you.'

As Mum launched into a lecture against astrology, I could see that Demi and Maryam were writing down their details, having clearly got them from their parents. Demi went over to Uri and I watched as he punched numbers into his computer and seconds later crisp sheets of paper were printed out and handed to her. He then took Maryam's and she got her horoscope too.

'Demi and Maryam's mums have given their details,' I said as soon as Mum paused to draw breath.

'Then they are very foolish.'

'Please, Mum. I'll wash up for a year.'

'Bargaining won't get you anywhere.'

'Two years.'

The phone went quiet for a few moments then I heard Mum laugh. 'Deal,' she said. 'You were born at 6 p.m. in the hospital just outside Bristol.' I knew she'd give in. She hated washing up. I realized back when I was about seven that I could use it as a bargaining tool.

'Thanks, Mum. You're a star. Oh, and can you give me Marcie's as well? I'll do the washing up forever.'

'Forever. You do realize that I will hold you to that, don't you? Now, Marcie? Ooh, let me think. She took a long time arriving, let me remember, yes, August 9th, about . . . about . . . 5.30 a.m.-ish. I can't quite remember.'

After the call, I clicked my phone shut and wrote down the details on the back of one of the leaflets I had picked up. When I got back to Uri, he was busy with a very loud family who were demanding their charts and giggling and generally making a big fuss.

He took Marcie's details, glanced at them, then shook his head. 'Hmm. And her fiancé is the Pisces?'

'Yes. Is there anything wrong with that?'

'I'll get back to you,' he said as the man from the loud family called him.

I felt so disappointed as I walked away. There was less than half an hour to go before the show finished and the family that was crowding around Uri looked like they could be there for at least that time. Demi and Maryam were studying their charts and looked well pleased with them. They wanted to go and sit down and get a drink while they looked at them properly. I went with them and we bought mango smoothies and sat down to read. Demi was Gemini with Libra rising.

'Maybe that's why we get on,' she said to me.

'And I am Sagittarius with Gemini rising,' Maryam said. 'Maybe that's why we get on, Demi.'

Demi nodded. 'The rest of it reads like gobbledegook, doesn't it?'

'Yeah,' said Maryam, and she folded her pages and put them in her bag. 'Way complicated.'

At the front of the hall, we could hear various prize-winners being called up on to the stage. We pulled our raffle tickets out from our pockets.

'There goes my silver limo,' said Maryam and she

tossed her tickets into the bin when the winner was announced to be number 202, Margaret Beesley.

'There goes my holiday in St Lucia,' said Demi and she tossed her tickets aside as another winner was announced.

Another few names were called and soon all our raffle tickets were in the bin.

Demi and Maryam sighed. 'Ah well, there's always next year,' I said.

'And now . . .' There was a burst of trumpets. 'Will Chloe Bradbury come to the stage area, please,' said a female voice over the loudspeakers.

'Ohmigod!' we chorused in unison.

I felt a rush of adrenalin. 'Maybe I've won something!' I looked in my purse to check for a stray ticket but they'd all gone. 'Oh no, I might have lost the ticket! I haven't got any left.'

'Chloe Bradbury, please come to the stage,' said the announcement again.

I was about to dive into the bin to retrieve the tickets we'd chucked away but Maryam and Demi hauled me out and towards the stage.

'Come on! Someone just called your name again. Let's go and see what you've got before they give your prize to someone else,' said Demi and she linked arms and pulled me towards the stage area.

Uri was standing mid-stage waiting for me. 'Come on,' he beckoned to me.

I'd grabbed Demi and Maryam's hands and pulled them up the steps with me but they pushed me forward to take my prize on my own.

'What have I won?' I whispered to Uri when I reached him.

He tapped the side of his nose and winked. As he did, the lights in the hall went down, bathing everyone in a soft pink glow. Soft spacey music began to play, a harp and tinkling bells. And then laser lights blasted on, swirling around the stage and the hall, and the space music grew more upbeat. Uri announced to the hall, 'Chloe Bradbury, YOU are this month's ZODIAC girl!'

From somewhere up high, white balloons were released. At that moment, the blonde woman who was the model in the goddess book stepped out from the left on to the stage. I recognized her straightaway. Nessa. I gasped. She really *did* look like a goddess and was even more beautiful in the flesh than in her photos. She was tall, with milky white skin, the most perfect heart-shaped face and sky-blue eyes, and she was dressed in one of her wedding dresses, a white off-the-shoulder sheath with one strap of tiny diamanté and the same lining the seams. The audience cheered and she waved back at them, every inch a celebrity.

She came over and placed a tiara on my head then put a white sash over my shoulders with the words ZODIAC GIRL written in silver sequins.

'Congratulations,' she said in a distinct Cockney accent and she handed me two blue boxes tied with silver ribbon.

I felt as if I was in a dream. On cloud nine. I could hardly breathe for excitement. In front of the stage, a sea of happy faces beamed back at me.

'Zodiac Girl? What does that mean?' I asked.

'Open your presents,' she said. 'You'll see.'

I untied the ribbon on the first box. Inside was a silver chain with a tiny charm with the symbol of the scales which I knew from my *Girl in the City* magazine represented Libra. Nessa took it from the box and put it around my neck while people cheered again. I opened the second box. Inside was the dinkiest mobile phone I had ever seen. It was turquoise with a beautiful opal stone above the dialling pad. To my right, Demi and Maryam gave me the thumbs up.

'Thank you,' I said to Nessa.

'You're welcome,' she replied. 'It's no ordinary phone. It's a *Zodiac* phone.' She gently ushered me to the wings of the stage and soon after, another prize-winner was announced and another person was making their way to the stage. Nessa indicated the phone. 'You're a very, very lucky girl. To be chosen to be a Zodiac Girl is a rare honour. For one month the stars will come to your aid and I, Nessa, the embodiment of Venus, will be your guardian. I will be there for you whenever you need. You can call on me or one of the other planets from your Zodiac phone. We are here for you for your special month and wish for you that it be magical and memorable.'

'Thank you,' I whispered although I had no idea what she had said. I was too busy gazing at her. I was completely star-struck. I had never met a celebrity before and my mind seemed to have gone blank.

The rest of the show felt like a blur. Nessa disappeared with Uri, people started packing up their stalls, and all too soon it was time to go home. Demi and Maryam were well impressed with my phone and pendant and both said how jealous they were that they hadn't been picked as Zodiac Girls.

'I'm going back to find that man,' said Maryam and she set off for Aisle H. Demi and I followed and we just caught Uri as he was about to leave on a unicycle.

'Hey, can we be Zodiac Girls too?' Maryam asked.

He shook his head. 'One month, one girl,' he said. Then he looked over at me and handed me a piece of paper. 'Here's your horoscope. Every month somewhere on the planet, according to the line-up of the stars, one girl, and one girl only, is chosen to be Zodiac

Girl. Mercury will be retrograde for your first week as Zodiac Girl. Mercury is the planet of communication. Hmm. With the line-up of stars in your chart, it could be tricky for the first seven days. Make sure you don't lose your phone. That's the sort of thing that happens when Mercury is going backwards. You have only been chosen for a month. But we'll be in touch if we can. In the meantime, Chloe, expect the unexpected. Toodles!' And with that, he rode off on his strange bike.

Chapter Three

Career Week

'Chloe, what can I put you down for?' asked Mr Mooney, our form teacher, on Monday morning.

'Um, art . . . um . . . English . . . um . . . when do we have to finally decide?'

Mr Mooney sighed. 'I was hoping today. Last week's homework, remember? Think about what you might like to do when you leave school, talk it over with your parents, come in ready with subject choices.'

I nodded. 'Sorry. Um . . . I thought I might do languages and then I changed my mind and thought, no, I like art and . . . oh, I can't decide! But it's not my fault – I'm a Libran. My star sign can never decide.'

'You're not the only one who knows about astrology, Chloe,' said Mr Mooney. 'I am a Taurus and we like to sit about watching television and eating good food, but do I give in to it? No. I come in to work and teach people like you. Do you see what I am saying? Sometimes you have to overcome some parts of your nature, so Libran or not, decide!'

So much for sympathy, I thought. All our teachers had been on about lately was what we wanted to do when we left school. Last week had been a special 'career week' with visiting speakers and talks in the lunch breaks. But get a job? What job? Go to college? To do what? Who knew? I certainly didn't and I was getting bored of everyone being so into it including Demi and Maryam, who were smug as bugs in rugs because they were well sorted and had their subjects choices picked, easy-peasy. I'd tried to keep an open mind and consider all the options but even after the endless lectures from visiting guests, I still wasn't any closer to knowing what to do. I'd gone from wanting to be a fashion designer with Demi to being a TV presenter, with lots of other options in between. Luckily Mr Mooney moved on from me.

'So let's hear some of your choices so far,' he said and he looked hopefully around the class.

Janice Aitkin put up her hand. 'An actress.'

Sophie Smith put up hers. 'Hairdresser, sir.'

Barbara Reilley called out. 'A teacher, sir.' She got a nod of approval for that but then she's always been teacher's pet.

Tracy Jones called out, 'Interior designer.'

Ellie Andrews, 'A holiday rep.'

'I'm not going to work at all,' said Susie Peterson. 'I'm going to marry dosh.'

Mr Mooney rolled his eyes. 'Good luck to you,' he said.

I was thinking, *How can they know? How can they be so sure? Even 'married to rich husband' is more than I can decide.*

'And what about you?' Mr Mooney asked Zoe Cain.

'Reality show celebrity,' she replied.

Mr Mooney sighed. 'Reality show celebrity isn't a career choice, Zoe.'

'Yes it is,' Zoe said. 'All you have to do is eat bugs or slugs in a remote jungle some place or get locked up in a house for a few weeks or have a big boob job and you could be set for life.'

Mr Mooney sighed again but the class laughed.

'Think again, Zoe,' said Mr Mooney. 'And you too, Susie Peterson.'

I was glad that I wasn't the only one who was being asked to rethink their plan. It was a difficult decision, a big choice, big pressure – what to do with the rest of our lives. Annoyingly, like the being a bridesmaid thing, everyone else seemed to be one step ahead of me. I've only ever wanted to be a bridesmaid and that's not exactly a serious career choice. When Mum walked into one of the meetings of the Bridesmaids' Club one month, she suggested that we start a band called the Bridesmaids. Sadly, even that wasn't an option because I'm tone deaf, Demi has the rhythm of a dead parrot, and although Maryam plays a musical instrument it's the ukulele, which even I know isn't rock and roll. While Mr Mooney moved on, I reached down to my rucksack and pulled out my Zodiac phone. With all the fun of the fair, I hadn't had a chance to look at it properly. I pressed the top to see if it switched on and seconds later, it bleeped that there was a message. And another. Mr Mooney swung round.

'Who's brought their phone into class?'

My desk is at the back and everyone turned round to look at me. Mr Mooney marched down the aisle and put his hand out. 'You know the rules, Bradbury. Hand me the phone.' I passed it over to him and he looked at it quizzically for a moment then went to the front of the class and put it in the drawer of his desk. 'You can have it back on Friday after school.'

Uri's words, 'Don't lose your phone,' echoed in my mind. Oops! So much for taking heed of his warning. I wasn't to know Mr Mooney would be on the warpath, but then Uri also said to expect the unexpected. Is this what he meant? Heck! I can't even contact him or Nessa to see what it's about. I put my forehead down on my desk and felt depressed for a few moments and then I remembered that I still had Marcie's wedding to organise. *You can't take that away from me, Mr Mooney! OK, so I don't know what I want to be or do but at least I have a wedding to look forward to!*

Chapter Four

Surprise!

On the Sunday afternoon that Marcie was due to visit, I had everything in my bedroom ready for her. I'd laid out fabric samples for dresses on the bed along with a variety of designs by Nessa. I put the latest *Wedding* magazines in a pile on my desk. I propped up photos of various bouquets by the wall, one with roses, one with freesias and one with white hyacinths, and I had a ton of others to show her if she didn't go for what I'd put out on display.

My plan was that after the obligatory catch-up with Mum, I would make Marcie and me a hot chocolate and then we could escape up to my room and get on with the business in hand. As I busied myself putting out everything I'd collected from the wedding show for her to look at, I felt a rush of excitement. *Life is just so brilliant*, I thought, as I fished out a pile of leaflets about limos and horse-drawn carriages.

This year's wedding show had been the best so far, not only because of the new stalls and getting the prize of being this month's Zodiac Girl there, but also because of meeting Nessa. I felt so happy as I remembered being the centre of attention for those few minutes up on stage. Nessa had said something about being my guardian and planet people being here to help me and I realized later that must mean that she and her colleagues would help me plan the perfect wedding. I guessed that being picked as a Zodiac Girl meant that I got the special promotions that were running for a month – I remembered Uri emphasizing something about the offer being for four weeks only. The Zodiac phone was clearly part of the Celestial Weddings marketing too because when I had got it back from Mr Mooney after school on Friday, I had tried putting in numbers of my friends and family but it didn't work. However, there were ten names and numbers on the address page already, all part of Celestial Weddings – some of them I recognized from the fair like Joe Jupiter, Uri and, of course, Nessa.

Very clever, to give out a phone with the names and numbers of all the aspects of the business. Much more imaginative than just using business cards, I thought as I glanced over the list again.

1) Nessa: Venus
2) Mr O: Sun
3) Mario: Mars

4) Hermie: Mercury
5) Joe: Jupiter
6) Captain John: Neptune
7) Dr Cronus: Saturn
8) Uri: Uranus
9) Selene: Moon.
10) PJ: Pluto.

Yes, they are all definitely part of Celestial Weddings, I decided, as they all had a planet after their name. If the standard of the rest of them was anything like as high as Nessa's designs and Joe Jupiter's fab food, we could hire the lot of them.

The Zodiac phone didn't work for phoning out normally. I tried dialling Demi's number but all I got was a voice telling me, 'Number not listed in address book.' I didn't mind that much because I already had a mobile and that worked fine although it wasn't as pretty. I moved from my desk the piles of potential courses and jobs brochures that the woman doing careers advice had left with me after the last session on Wednesday and replaced them with lovely wedding mags. I still wasn't any clearer about what I wanted to do despite the growing pressure to think about subject choices but I wasn't going to worry about that today.

I heard the doorbell go and raced down, to find Marcie at the front door. She looked great, with a new haircut in soft layers around her face. I could just imagine it tied up with freesias wound into it, or maybe jasmine – the small star-shaped flowers would really stand out against her chestnut-coloured hair. I'd let her decide.

'Congratulations!' I said, and went and gave her a hug. She grinned back, put her arms around me and we did a skip around whilst still hugging.

Mum came out from the back room. An older version of Marcie with the same dark hair and amber eyes. She joined in the hug. 'Chloe's been researching your wedding while you've been away,' she said when we pulled back. 'I trust that you are still getting married? Haven't changed your mind on the plane back?' *Always the same*, I thought. *All my family are doubtful that anything can ever work out.* I was about to say something but bit it back. I didn't want to ruin Marcie's good news moment by arguing with Mum. 'No,' said Marcie. 'We've even fixed a date. June 15th, we thought.'

I punched the air. 'Yay. You'll be a summer bride. Fab. I've got loads of stuff to show you, Marce.'

Marcie smiled, sort of – it was a cross between a smile and a wince. *Oh poor thing*, I thought, *she's worried already. Everyone knows how stressful it is being a bride but she has me. I will make it easy-peasy.*

'Lunch in five,' Mum said. 'Table's set. Marcie,

come and chat while I set the table. How's Geoff? I thought you might have brought him along.'

Marcie looked uncomfortable and shifted about from foot to foot. 'Ah yes. Geoff. I have something to tell you about him.'

We followed Mum into the kitchen and Marcie sat at the table while Mum and I found cutlery.

'OK, I'm just going to come out and say it,' Marcie blurted. 'Um, Geoff. Yes. We broke up.'

'You *what?*' I was horrified. 'When?'

'A few weeks ago. Just before we were meant to go to Paris.'

'Before Paris?' I said. 'But you spoke to me. I don't understand. So the wedding's off?'

'Yes. No. I mean yes, it's off with Geoff. I broke up with him before I went away.'

Mum looked as puzzled as I was. 'So what about the engagement?' she asked. 'What do you mean you broke up before you went away, Marcie love? You mean after, surely.' Mum glanced at me. 'She's clearly upset and got all her dates mixed up.'

Marcie took a deep breath. 'No, I haven't. I broke up with Geoff before I went away. Listen, he just wasn't right, that is, he was so right, he looked great, he was great but . . . but . . . the chemistry wasn't there. I was going to tell you but . . . I knew that you all liked him and I didn't want you talking me out of it.'

'But what about Paris? The proposal?' I asked. 'You said June 15th for the wedding date when you came in.'

Marcie nodded. 'Yes. It is. And I did get engaged. That part is right.'

'But you just said you broke up with Geoff,' I said. 'I'm confused.'

'I did break up with Geoff. And I did get engaged. To Sam. I got engaged to Sam.'

'Sam!' Mum and I chorused and we both sat down with a thud.

Marcie nodded. 'He got in touch a couple of nights before I went to Paris and begged me not to go. He said his life had been a misery without me, and just hearing his voice made me realize how much I'd missed him. I'd been going out with Geoff on the rebound and it wasn't fair to him, to keep stringing him along when I knew the magic ingredient wasn't there and all along I was still in love with Sam. I didn't think Sam would ever settle down so there was no point, but he's changed, and says he's realized that he can't live without me. When he came over, I realized in a second that all the old feelings were still there and in fact had never really gone away.'

'Sam?' I repeated. I couldn't take it in. Mum didn't

seem too upset, she'd always liked Sam, and she got up and finished setting the table and served lunch while she pressed Marcie for more details. I sat between them doing my goldfish impersonation. I was in shock as I listened while she told the whole story. I couldn't get my head around it. Sam? *Sam?*

It turned out that Marcie never went to Paris. Instead Sam took her to a B. & B. in Bognor Regis. He proposed over breakfast. Hid the ring in a muffin. I couldn't help feeling disappointed. It was supposed to have been Paris, one of the most romantic cities in the world. There were so many fabulous locations that Sam could have chosen – a city in Spain or Italy, a beach in Morocco or even Cornwall, a balcony with a view, a sunset, a lovely moment to remember – not a breakfast table laid with salt, pepper, maybe a tomato sauce bottle and a muffin in blooming Bognor Regis. Sam? *Sam?* Pff! He had never struck me as someone who had much romance in his soul. Marcie was lucky she hadn't got the ring attached to a pair of sneakers.

'You OK, Chloe?' asked Marcie.

'Nff, yes, no. Just a bit of a shock, that's all. I . . . thought we were going to be welcoming Geoff into the family and now, er . . . Are you absolutely sure, Marcie? I mean, you broke up with Sam.'

'I have never been so sure about anything in my life.

I love him. I always have. I broke up with him because he wouldn't commit to a wedding – you remember how he feels about them – but he told me that the months without me had been a complete misery and he'd do anything to have me back, even get married. I know he means it this time. I know he's The One.'

I knew I mustn't put a damper on her happiness but my heart was sinking. *I mustn't let it show*, I thought. 'Um. Tell me about the proposal again,' I said.

She blushed slightly while she repeated the story, then she showed us her ring. Diamond. Classic. Not too flashy. *Bit ordinary*, I thought. *A more modern design would have looked better*. But then Sam was a bloke. A *blokey* bloke. He couldn't be relied on to be up on the latest engagement jewellery.

'Are you quite quite *quite* sure?' I asked again.

'Chloe! Anyone would think that you're not happy for me. Don't you like Sam?' Marcie retorted.

'Um, yes, course,' I said. 'He's . . . very handsome.' He was. No denying that.

'He always thought you didn't like him,' said Marcie. 'Please say you do, Chloe. For me. I know he made fun of the Bridesmaids' Club but he's a real sweetie deep down. He wants you to like him and I so want you to get on.'

I didn't want to ruin her day. *I will do my best*, I thought, but looking at Marcie's finger and the ordinary ring made me more resolute than ever to get the rest of the wedding right. 'If you like him, then I like him,' I said in the most convincing way that I could muster up. I didn't say that I liked Geoff more.

After we'd cleared up the dishes, I finally managed to steal Marcie away.

'Wow! You've been busy,' she said as she surveyed my room.

I pushed aside a pile of magazines to make space for her on my bed. 'I have. I've already done a lot of sifting through and eliminated a lot of the dross so we only have the best ideas to look at. I met the most *amazing* new people at the fair. I think we should hire all of them.'

Again a worried expression crossed Marcie's face. Not so much a smile as a wince. I took her hand. 'Hey, it's going to be all right. If you think that Sam is the right man for you then I will do my best to get on better with him. And we're going to make you the most perfect wedding, don't you worry.' I meant it too – I'd compromise on the groom as long as I got my chance to be a bridesmaid.

'Thanks, Chloe, and of course I will look at what you've picked out. It's just . . . well . . . Sam and I talked about it when we were away . . .'

I passed her the first bunch of brochures to look at.

'Great,' I said. 'It's always good to get input from the groom. We want everyone to be happy.'

She reached into the pocket of her jeans and pulled out a slip of paper. 'Well,' she said. 'You know how Sam thinks that weddings are basically just a piece of paper, so I agreed to compromise on the ceremony and have some . . . er, fun. We decided, or that is, these are mainly Sam's ideas, they are . . . um . . . a bit different.'

I took the piece of paper. 'Good. Different is good. We don't want your wedding to be like any other and I am sure it won't be. Oh Marcie, I have met the most awesome woman. She does dresses and make-up and . . .' I glanced at the list and did a double take. I read it again. I laughed. 'Oh, very good, Marcie. Very funny. You almost got me there for a moment.' I sat next to her. 'And how long have you been planning this little joke?'

Marcie wasn't laughing. 'Not a joke. It will be fun but I'm serious about it. We want our day to be a day to remember and Sam thought if we picked something on that list, it would be.'

I looked back at the list. Marcie's wedding suggestions were:

1) Roller-skate wedding
2) Velcro wedding

3) Bungee-jump wedding
4) Underwater wedding
5) Bridezilla wedding with bride and groom dressed as gorillas.

Oh. My. God! I thought as my mind filled with horror and my heart sank. It couldn't be true.

'You're really serious?'

Marcie nodded. 'Serious.'

'But these ideas are mad,' I said. I glanced back down at the list. Sam's input? What about my input? Years of it? But no, Sam was the groom. He had first say. *Oh Geoff, come back. Where are you?* I thought. I glanced up at Marcie again and wished that she loved him, not Sam.

'But what about all the work I've done? I've been planning this for years!'

A flash of irritation crossed Marcie's face. She stood up and her cheeks flushed pink. 'My wedding, Chloe. *My* wedding. Mine and Sam's, so we have first say. You could have at least tried to understand but no, you just want it your way. You aren't happy that the man I love has asked me to marry him, and you can't hide it, not even for me.' She looked close to tears as she stood up and went to the door where she turned back to look at me. 'You are the most selfish person,

Chloe, and you're only thinking of yourself and what you want in all of this.'

She went out and slammed the door behind her. I was stunned. Marcie never lost it. Jane and Clare yes, but not Marcie. I heard her stomp down the stairs and then the front door banged shut. I lay back on my bed and burst into tears. It wasn't fair. I had only wanted the wedding plans to be lovely for everyone – that wasn't selfish. How could she accuse me of that? I only wanted everything to be beautiful for her. Oh rotten bananas! *Am I feeling bad because I want my own way?* I wondered. *Oh poo! This is so not how it was meant to be.*

Chapter Five

Arghhhh!

After Marcie had gone, I picked up Sergeant Ted, my favourite teddy bear, from his place on my bed, cuddled up to him, then sat and stared at the phone. I wanted to call Demi or Maryam and tell them the awful news about Marcie marrying Sam and their mad wedding plans but I wasn't ready for their reaction. They were bound to laugh because the whole idea was ridiculous.

I put away my bridesmaid album, stacked all the magazines and brochures and put them in the bottom of the cupboard next to the boring career leaflets, then stared out of the window. I felt shocked. Numb. Not one of the options on Marcie's list had featured in my album. Not *one*. I felt like lying on the floor and having a temper tantrum like a three-year-old. *I planned for everything except this*, I said to myself. A sound like wind chimes rang out and on the bedside cabinet, my Zodiac phone began to vibrate and move until it fell on to the carpet. I picked it up and pressed a green button that was flashing

'Awright, Chloe,' said Nessa. 'Nessa 'ere.'

'Oh, hi, Nessa,' I said. 'So it does work.'

'What? The phone? Course. It's for me and you to stay in touch. I've been looking at your chart and there's a lot of stuff going on for you at the moment, unsettling for you. I thought you might 'ave rung already.'

'Chart? Rung you? About the wedding?'

'No. Because you're our Zodiac Girl this month and I'm 'ere to 'elp.'

'I couldn't even if I'd thought of it. One of my teachers confiscated my phone last Monday so I only got it back on Friday night and anyway, I didn't think I could phone out on it.'

I could hear Nessa tut. 'Course, Mercury was retrograde – that always messes up communications. Unfortunate when that 'appens in a Zodiac month – it means we can't always reach you, but at least it was only for a week and now we're back on track. We never know exactly how Mercury goin' retrograde is going to manifest – computers break down, Internet access gets lost, phone batteries go flat, that sort of thing, but with you, yer teacher took the phone. Ah well, what's done is done. You'll get other opportunities.'

I had no idea what Nessa was on about.

'Opportunities? To do what?' I asked.

'To be your very best self. To be who you're meant to be.'

Her words made me feel more depressed than ever. Be who I was supposed to be? That was my other problem. Nessa seemed to pick up on my thoughts. 'And that's another thing, Nessa. At school we are supposed to know what we want to do when we're older and I haven't got a clue! I don't know what I want to do or who I want to be. God! Life stinks. I keep changing my mind about everything.'

'Your chart said you 'ad a difficult time comin'. Neptune, that's the planet of dreams, crossed by Pluto and Saturn. Tough going, doll.'

'Are they two more of your colleagues in the wedding business?'

'Yes, but they're also planets in your chart and they're set against each other at a difficult angle.'

'I don't know much about astrology, Nessa. In fact, I don't know what you mean at all.'

'Saturn is the taskmaster of the Zodiac. When it's crossed or at a difficult angle in your chart, it means a lesson to be learned. Pluto is the planet of transformation. It can descend to the roots of your ideas and shake them up. Put those two at a tricky angle to Neptune—'

51

'The planet of dreams.'

'That's it. You're getting it. Put those three together and I'd say that some dream of yours 'as been shaken or shattered.'

I still wasn't sure what she was on about and why she had to bring planets into it all the time but maybe that was her thing, her way of expressing herself. Whatever – she seemed to have grasped that things had gone wrong. 'Tell me about it. Shaken *and* shattered, Nessa. And not some dream – my *life's* dream.'

'Did you get my text?'

'Yes. Um, not to resist or something.'

'Exactly,' said Nessa. 'Listen, sweet'eart, you 'ave to ride this next bit of your life like you're surfin' a wave, a tidal wave. Don't fight what's 'appenin'. You gotta go with it.'

'But Nessa, everything's gone wrong and now my sister hates me.'

'Why? What's 'appened?'

'My sister Marcie is getting married to an idiot who thinks that weddings are a joke. He's going to turn theirs into one and I'm going to be the laughing stock of the school. I had it all planned and wanted to use your designs and your friends in the planet company too but I am sorry, it's not going to happen.'

''Ey, I'm not 'ere to sell you my business,' said Nessa. 'I'm here to 'elp.'

That's sweet, I thought and I sniffed back a tear. 'OK. Listen to this then.' I read Marcie's list. I heard a soft laugh at the other end.

'See? I *knew* people would laugh and I don't blame you. And now I know I can't ever tell my friends. Marcie didn't even glance at half the stuff I had looked out for her and now she hates me and thinks that I'm selfish, which is so not fair because all I have been doing these last weeks is thinking about her.'

'Chloe love, could be that this is what you bein' Zodiac Girl is all about. You're one of the luckiest girls on the planet. Some of the most famous women in history were Zodiac Girls. Marie Curie, Cleopatra, Elizabeth the First – she was one but . . . Are you cryin', doll?'

'No.'

'Chloe. Chloe. Gawd! You girls never get it at first, do ya? Listen. 'Elp is at 'and.'

'Nothing could 'elp, I mean help. Not unless you know Marcie or Sam and can talk them out of this.'

'This isn't about them. It's about *you*. You. It could be the time of your life. A time that affects everythin'. See, it doesn't 'appen to just any girl. It 'appens to a girl when she's at a turnin' point in 'er life. It's not always clear at first why a girl 'as been chosen as Zodiac Girl and it's really up to each girl to make of it what she will. What we 'ave to work out is why you've

53

been chosen, what you're meant to get out of it. I reckon this big let-down of yours is part of it. It may not be as bad as you think.'

'My sister dressed as a gorilla or bungee-jumping instead of floating down the aisle in one of your beautiful creations! How much worse than that could it get?'

Nessa laughed again. 'Yeah. Not quite your dreamy gorgeous wedding. But what you 'ave to remember is that nothin' is set in stone. Want to know one of my favourite sayings?'

I was feeling so miserable that I didn't really but I knew it would be rude not to say yes. 'Yes. What is it? Darkest hour is just before dawn?'

'No. Although that is a good 'un. My favourite saying is 'What you resist, persists'. Good lesson in life that, Chloe, if you really get it. What I am sayin' is, go along with your sister's plans. Try not to resist. In fact, try to enjoy it even. It's your 'alf term next week. It just so 'appens that we offer those kind of alternative weddings as well as the traditional ones, and so as part of your prize you could come along and try them out for free – a different option on the list each day. Could be fun.'

Fun? I thought. *Are you kidding?*

'You 'ave to let 'er explore 'er options,' said Nessa.

54

'These aren't options, they're catastrophes,' I groaned as I threw the list into the bin.

'Remember the golden rule, that's all I'm goin' to ask you for now. What you resist, persists, so go along with your sister and *enjoy* it.'

I liked Nessa and I wanted her to like me so I decided to agree. 'OK. Maybe.'

'Good girl. And we'll be in touch, yeah? Nil desperandum.'

'Yeah, right. Nil desperwotsit. Whatever.'

Nessa laughed then hung up. I picked the list out of the bin and glanced at it again. *What can I do?* I asked myself. *Stamp my foot like a spoilt princess, blub myself sick and force Marcie to do what I wanted no matter what? That wasn't an option either.* I got up and kicked the wall. 'Ow! That hurt!' I groaned as my toe throbbed big time. 'But . . . *God*, life stinks sometimes,' I said to Sergeant Ted. 'It's so hard when the one thing you've always wanted doesn't turn out the way you expect. Is this how it's going to be from now on? Let-down after let-down? Will I spend my entire life staggering from one disappointment to another? Will *nothing* turn out as planned?'

Sergeant Ted didn't reply. He's a bear of few words.

'Don't look at me like that,' I said to him. 'I know, I know. Nessa was right. I'll ring Marcie and say that I'll give it a go. OK?'

I swear Sergeant Ted nodded at the same time as my Zodiac phone bleeped that I had a message, then another, then another.

One was from Nessa:

Uranus is square to Mars and Saturn in your chart and at a tricky angle to Neptune and Pluto. I said it was going to be a difficult time! However Venus is conjunct with Mercury at a favourable angle so there will be a bit of a reprieve and a harmonious time coming up too, probably tomorrow.

She was right about the difficult time, I thought as I checked the second message, which was from Uri. He had written,

A friend is someone who knows your secret dream and holds your hand when it shatters.

On a good day, I might have thought his words were way soppy like blurgh, vomit, but at that moment, they touched me. *That's so true*, I thought. I always shared everything with Maryam and Demi, good and bad. We had always been there for each other – like when Maryam's dad was ill last summer and she was so upset, and last term when Demi liked a boy in Year Ten and he went off with Tania Cosgrave and she was gutted. We had always sworn to be there for each other. I shouldn't cut them out now because I was afraid that they might laugh. *Spot on, Uri,* I thought. *Friends are for rain and shine.*

The third message was from Nessa again and it said:

the Sun is well aspected to Mercury next week. Enjoy.

More planet gobbledegook. Nessa really is into it, I thought as I picked up my normal mobile phone to send a text to Demi and Maryam. All it said was SOS. Those were our code words for help needed and fast. Dad had told me ages ago that SOS were letters used by ships if they were in danger, and if the message was received by anyone they would write WILCO back, which means, 'Got your message and will comply.'

Two minutes after I had sent the message, I had two texts back saying WILCO.

Twenty minutes later, Maryam and Demi were at the door with a bag of jelly beans and a bag of dolly mixture (both my all-time faves).

Chapter Six

Option One

'You ready?' Marcie called up the stairs.

'Coming,' I called back from my bedroom where I had been getting ready with Demi and Maryam. It was a freezing day outside, cold, grey and misty, and I had pulled out all the scarves, gloves and woolly hat sets that my gran had knitted for me over the years and put them on the bed for my mates to wear. Maryam had chosen a turquoise set, mine was pink and Demi's was scarlet. We were about to leave when I changed my mind and thought that maybe pale blue would be nicer for today.

Demi took the blue one and shoved it back in my drawer. 'Pink. Pink. *Pink!* If we wait for you to decide, we'll be here all day. You know what you're like.'

I let her boss me about sometimes because she was right. Some days I would agonize over the smallest decisions. We all stood in the model pose that we had learned from one of Demi's fashion mags – body turned left side forward, left hip dropped, shoulders and face facing forward, then checked our reflections in the mirror. 'We may only be going roller skating,' I said in a silly posh voice, 'but we should *never* forget our sense of style.'

We did our club's sign to each other, left thumbs up, down, up, then jostled each other out into the hall and downstairs to meet Marcie.

'And so the half term begins,' she said as she ushered us out of the door and into her Volkswagen Polo.

'So how does this roller-skating wedding thing work?' asked Demi once we were in the back of the car and on our way. I did love her and Maryam. They'd been brilliant when I'd broken the news to them about Marcie's list and they hadn't laughed, at least not until I got to the Bridezilla option when they did crack up for a few seconds. They had understood straight away how upset I was and had done their best to cheer me up. As members of the Bridesmaids' Club, both of them insisted on coming with me to research the list and somehow it didn't seem so depressing knowing that they would be there, especially for the roller skating. I am rubbish at it – have been ever since I was seven and got a pair of skates for Christmas and our dog Boris was more excited by them than I was. Every time I got my balance and skated off, he'd run after me, jump up and flatten me. Over and over again. Being bruised and battered again as a bridesmaid didn't hold much appeal but I think Marcie had conveniently forgotten about my earlier disasters. She was so happy when I called late last night and said I'd be happy to try out her list with her.

'The idea is that the ceremony is conducted by a vicar on skates in a park in the centre of town. The bride, the groom and guests would strap on skates and skate along behind him to that lovely pergola by the fountain.'

'What, even Grandma?' I asked. 'No way will she be able to skate.'

'Oh God! You're right,' Marcie replied. 'I hadn't thought of the old ones. Er . . . OK, so maybe just a few of us can do the skating thing.'

One point against, I clocked up inwardly when I saw a flicker of doubt register on Marcie's face. *Maybe this isn't going to be as hard as I thought!*

'I think you should give people the choice,' I said. 'I mean, not everyone, no matter what their age, can skate. Like, remember Boris?'

'Boris?'

'Yes. Boris. Our dog. Remember when I was little? He jumped up whenever I put skates on and sent me flying over and over again. I will give it a go today but I am not very good at it.'

'Oh Chloe! I am so sorry. I had completely forgotten about that. Er . . . you don't have to do it if you don't want. In fact, maybe it should be just me and Sam and the vicar.' Marcie looked even more worried.

Two points against, I thought. *This is going to be so easy. Nessa was right. Don't resist and things may work out after all.*

'How did you know that Sam was The One and not Geoff?' Demi asked.

'Oh, the way I feel when I'm with him,' Marcie replied. 'Kind of tingly all over, light-headed—'

'That's how I feel when I get flu,' I interrupted and Demi and Maryam cracked up. 'Sorry, Marcie – couldn't resist. But surely it must be more than that?'

'If you'd let me finish!' said Marcie, but she was smiling so I knew she didn't mind being teased. 'I feel comfortable with him, more comfortable than with any other man I've been out with, and I can't wait to see him again. I love spending time with him. Geoff was a nice guy, maybe too nice – but the spark just wasn't there the way it is with Sam.'

'So how come he's managed to bully you into trying out all these wacky weddings, Marcie? I just don't get it. When you were younger you always planned to have a traditional wedding. What's made you change your mind?'

'I . . . er . . . A relationship is about compromise, Chloe. About listening to the other's point of view. About sharing.'

'But he's left you to check out all the wedding options,' I said. 'Why's he not sharing doing this?'

'My mum says you have to start a marriage the way you intend to continue,' added Demi, 'and that's by sharing the chores.'

'Did you tell him that you wanted a traditional wedding?' asked Maryam.

'Not exactly,' said Marcie, then she was quiet for a while. 'And he couldn't get out of his commitments this week – he had to take a group of students rambling and he had just taken the week off to be with me,' she said finally, but for the rest of the journey, she looked reflective and I wondered if our comments had touched a nerve.

When we got to the park, Marcie stopped the car and we got out and looked about but there didn't appear to be anybody around, just a woman walking her dog and a man eating a sandwich on a bench.

'The representative said she'd meet us here,' said Marcie.

'At least it's stopped raining,' Demi commented as

she looked around at the grass, which was still wet from the earlier downpour.

'Might that be the representative?' asked Maryam as a large woman in a violet tracksuit came roller-blading (or rather roller-blundering) down the path towards us.

'Omigod!' I heard Marcie say under her breath. The woman did look a sight, huffing and puffing to keep her balance, clearly not a natural on the skates. I glanced at Demi and Maryam, who had fixed bright expressions on their faces. I could tell that they were dying to laugh. *Phew!* I thought as she skated past. *Not her then.*

I shot Demi and Maryam a glance. Demi raised her right eyebrow. I knew we were all thinking the same thing – that the whole idea of a roller-skate wedding was tack city.

He came out of nowhere. A skater. A flash of silver against the grey morning, flying by as if he had winged feet.

'Wow!' we chorused as the silver blur turned and skated back towards us, slowing down as he approached.

'Double wow!' said Demi.

'Triple that,' said Maryam.

The skater was a babe. Tall and athletic, he was dressed in a silver padded jumpsuit, the kind that people wear to go skiing, and he had shoulder-length brown wavy hair. It was hard to tell how old he was, maybe eighteen, but his eyes looked older, wiser, as though he had seen something of life. He had perfect skin, a square jaw and cheekbones to die for and I felt my knees turn to jelly as he bowed, flashed us a killer watt smile, did a quick spin on his skates then took off his backpack.

'Hi, I'm Hermie.'

'Nuf, ki . . . yeah,' I stuttered.

'Kee, yud, ee,' said Demi.

'Yom,' said Maryam.

'Werd . . .' said Marcie.

I giggled. We all seemed to be suffering from the same lack of mouth-to-brain coordination. Hermie smiled. Being the total love god that he was, he was probably used to girls falling apart in front of him.

'I'm Hermie, part of the Celestial Weddings company,' he said. 'I'm waiting for my partner. She'll be along in a short while. Want to try out while we wait?'

'Yes!' we chorused. Even I was excited now. Hermie reached into his backpack and pulled out four pairs of silver skates, which he handed out. We sat down on the bench and put them on – they all fitted perfectly, although I didn't remember telling anyone our sizes. I glanced at Demi and Maryam, who were both blushing and stealing glances at Hermie. When we were ready, he skated in front of Marcie and held out his hands to her. She reached for him and he pulled her up, let go and off she went. Next Hermie pulled up Demi, then Maryam, and they skated off too. I fiddled with my laces.

'Ready?' asked the love god.

'Um, I'm not very good at skating.'

'Bad experience when you were little, huh?'

'How did you know?'

'Was in your birth chart. When you were about seven?'

'But . . . huh . . . how did you know?'

'Friend of Nessa's. You're the Zodiac Girl, right?'

'Yes. Although I'm not completely sure what that means.'

Hermie held his hands out to me. 'It means be brave! Have the time of your life. Come on. Give it a go.'

I really wanted him to like me and I didn't want him to think I was a coward so when he grasped my hands I wobbled to my feet, and once upright he pushed me off, then skated on to check on the others. I skated along as best as I could, holding on to the backs of park benches, litter bins – whatever I could hang on to. Suddenly the path became a downhill slope. I could see Hermie and the others glide down and steady up as the path became level again at the bottom. I took a deep breath and skated down. Not good! I lost control completely and sped towards a duck pond, wailing my head off.

'WARGHHH! Help!'

Hermie sped back to my rescue, grabbed my waist, and slowed me down to a speed that was slightly less terrifying.

'Don't let go,' I panted.

'I won't,' he said and he took my hands and skated backwards while I skated forwards.

'OK?' he asked.

'Wurgh.' It took a moment but I realized that I was skating really well. 'Actually, yeah! But don't let go, will you?'

'Promise I won't. Now relax. Take three deep breaths. In, blow out. In, blow out. In, blow out.'

I did as I was told and felt a bit better.

'So, Zodiac Girl. What do you know about astrology?' asked Hermie.

'Not much. I'm a Libran. Demi's Gemini. Maryam's Sagittarius. I know a bit about Librans now – like we're lovers of beauty, um . . . don't like being rushed . . .'

'Which is probably why roller-skating wasn't your favourite thing,' said Hermie. 'But you're doing very well and relaxing into it. Did you know that each sign has a ruling planet?'

'Ish. Nessa said something about it.'

'Librans are ruled by Venus. That's Nessa. My name is Hermie and I'm Mercury, the planet of communication, which rules Virgo and Gemini.'

'I saw that all the branches of Celestial Weddings are named after planets. I think that's so cool.'

Hermie looked at me intently, then he sighed. 'Anyway. Did you know that Mercury is also known as the winged messenger?'

'No, but that's a good name for you. You skate as if you have winged feet.'

Hermie laughed. 'My thing is mainly to do with communication though. Nessa told me that you were freaked about your sister's wedding plans.'

'They did come out of the blue.'

'That would have been because of Uranus in your chart. When it features, it brings the unexpected, like a bolt of lightning.'

'Exactly.'

'But you're coping well. That's because essentially Libra is an easy-going sign—'

'Yes, and I hate it when people don't get along.'

'What I'd like to communicate to you,' Hermie continued, 'is to see both sides. Think you can do that? Should be easy for a Libran.'

'See that my ideas were fab and hers are insane?' I asked. 'Easy.'

Hermie laughed and shook his gorgeous mane of hair as we glided along at a gentle pace. 'All you have to do is to let go of the way you want things for just the rest of your month as Zodiac Girl. See it as an adventure and enjoy the ride.'

I had to admit that skating with one of the most handsome boys on the planet was quite enjoyable. I let go, and then it felt amazing, like I was floating along. I dared to glance to my side, and saw that Demi, Marcie and Maryam were doing really well, all confident skaters. We skated to the end of the path and stopped.

'Oh, here comes Nessa,' said Hermie. He pointed to the top of the hill. I turned and at that moment the clouds parted and a ray of sun shone down like a spotlight on the part of the path where Nessa stood, resplendent in a beautiful white skating outfit trimmed with fake fur, her hair wound up into a delicate crown that looked as if it was made from icicles. She looked every inch a snow queen and I was mesmerized. She skated down to join Hermie and together they held hands and continued along the path. They were totally in step with each other, graceful and elegant. To their left I could see that Demi, Maryam and Marcie had stopped skating and like me, were watching the performance. An image began to form in my mind despite all my former resistance. Marcie in a similar outfit trimmed with diamanté, a tiara on her head. She'd glide to the outdoor altar. Sam in black beside her. Behind them, Demi, Maryam and me in tiny silver skirts like cheerleaders. We could even work out a skating routine. It needn't be tacky at all. It could be the talk of the year. 'So innovative. So daring,' the guests would say. I'd certainly never seen anything like it in any of the wedding magazines. We could be the first. Could it be a possibility? *No, no*, I thought, *I mustn't let myself be persuaded.* However, Nessa must have picked up on my thoughts because she skated over to me.

'Could be lovely, couldn't it?' she asked.

'Maybe.'

'Everything in life is what you make of it. Harmony or disaster, it's your choice.'

I was about to tell her that in that case my choice would still be a traditional wedding where Marcie looked like a classic beautiful bride, when the woman who had clumsily skated past earlier came huffing along the path. She looked Nessa and Hermie up and down with disapproval. 'Lesson number one, my dears,' she barked. 'Outfits like that won't do, you know. You'll catch your death. Thermal vests, that's what you need.' And with that, she skated off again, leaving us trying not to laugh.

Marcie skated up behind us. 'Thank you so much,' she said to Hermie and Nessa. 'All very impressive.'

Behind her Nessa gave me the thumbs up, but even though they'd made it look lovely I wasn't going to let myself be convinced *that* easily.

In the car going home, I gave it some serious thought. It wasn't what I wanted for Marcie or myself, not by a long shot, but maybe it wasn't as bad as I had first imagined. 'If you do go for it,' I said, 'we'd better have a covered aisle in case it rains, and we have to make it clear that the oldies don't have to do it.'

'Yes, of course,' said Marcie. 'And it was fun, wasn't it?'

'Ish,' I said.

'I think it could be great,' said Demi. 'We just need to make sure we have the right outfits. Something like Hermie and Nessa were wearing.'

'Exactly,' said Maryam. 'Cutie cute.'

Marcie looked thoughtful. 'Yes, but it's only option one. We have others to try and you may have been right in the beginning, Chloe. It might be risky and I don't want a wedding where we have to call in the paramedics if anyone was to fall.'

'Calling in the paramedics needn't be a problem,' said Demi. 'They could be on skates too. It would be a whole production. Hermie and Nessa could be on the guest list too in case you needed any skating backup.'

'I guess,' said Marcie, but I could see that she was worried about broken bones and old aunties and uncles. By the time we had got home, I got the feeling that option one might be struck from the list.

Chapter Seven

Velcro!

'So what's number two on the list?' I asked when I got into the car the next morning. I'd wrapped up warm because once again the day was wet and grey. This time, it was just Marcie and me because Maryam and Demi had both been hauled off to spend 'quality' time with their families. None of us were keen on 'quality' time because it usually involved us getting a lecture of some sort about homework or bad behaviour or in my case, what subjects I should choose and what I wanted to be when I was older. I still didn't know despite spending ages browsing the career option brochures last night before I went to bed.

Marcie's worries seemed to have evaporated overnight and she was in a positive mood again. 'I think this one is going to be great,' she said. 'It's the Incredible Velcro wedding. I'm not sure what happens exactly.'

'Their slogan could be "You'll be stuck for life",' I joked.

Marcie laughed. 'Oh, very good. And Chloe, I want you to know that I do appreciate you coming with me to do this. I know Sam would have liked to come with us but as you know, he had things to do so it's up to me and thee. Just like old times, hey? I know it's not what you had in mind for me but I think it's fantastic that you are willing to give it a go.' I wasn't sure if it was wishful thinking on my part but I thought I detected a hint of regret when she said that it wasn't what I had in mind for her. Maybe there was room for persuasion to bring her back to her senses at a later date. Today, I was taking Nessa's and Hermie's advice and taking the path of least resistance, trying to see it as an adventure and to enjoy it.

Nessa had called just before I had set out and said that she might see me later – something to do with Uranus and Venus in my chart. Uranus was Uri. I was beginning to get the hang of her colleagues in the wedding business and their nicknames within it. All I had to do was look on my Zodiac phone and they were listed on there. Hermie was down as Mercury, Nessa as Venus, Uri, Uranus – I explained it all to Marcie and like me, she thought it was a great idea as a marketing concept.

She followed the directions to the Velcro wedding centre and after a short drive we ended up in what looked like an industrial estate. I felt my heart sink – it was the most unglamorous location I had ever seen. No trees, just concrete buildings covered in graffiti, warehouses with broken windows, what was once a giant carpet market but was now empty and boarded up, and that was it. Definitely not a place to bring a wedding party.

'Are you sure you have the right place?' I asked as I got out of the car and pulled my jacket tight around me. I didn't like the look of the location at all – it had a menacing feel about it and the enthusiasm I'd mustered the previous day was fast disappearing. *Roller-skating with a love god, maybe*, I thought. *Getting married in Velcro, I am not so sure.*

'I have to call a number when we arrive,' said Marcie, looking at her slip of paper, 'and someone will come out to meet us.'

'Does Mum know that we're here?' I asked as I noticed dark alleyways at the sides of the buildings and a pile of broken bottles and rubbish blowing about in the wind.

Marcie laughed. 'Why? Do you think we might disappear?'

I nodded and Marcie laughed again but her laughter was hollow. I could see that she didn't like the place any more than I did. A gust of wind sent wrappers and papers into the air. I had a bad feeling. 'Let's go home,' I suggested.

Marcie nodded and we were about to get into the car when a dark figure appeared down the alleyway. I felt my heart leap into my mouth as he began to approach us. 'Quick,' I said to Marcie. 'Someone's there.'

We leaped into the car and Marcie slammed the locks shut and started the engine. The man in shadow came into view. He was tall and thin and dressed from head to toe in black. He came over to the car and Marcie wound the window down.

'You come for the Velcro wedding?' he asked, revealing an uneven set of yellow teeth.

Marcie nodded.

'Come on then, you're late,' said the man. 'I'm Don Waters and I'll be the guide – least for now I will be.' He beckoned us to get out and set off for the warehouse. I noticed that he walked with a slight limp.

'We'd better go,' said Marcie, 'in case there's some kind of cancellation fee.'

'But I can tell already that this will be a no without us even having to go in. Can't you?' I said as we got out of the car to follow him.

'We can cut it short and then be off,' Marcie agreed.

Don led us down the alley, into a side door then into a dark corridor. He flicked a switch and a fluorescent light just about lit up our way. I glanced up and saw a bulb so covered in dust and cobwebs that it barely gave out any light. Don opened a door and we found ourselves in the open space of a warehouse. Another light was switched on and in the corner I saw an enormous trampoline. Don pointed at it. 'That's where you'll be. I'll show you what to do but I don't do it myself any more.' He indicated his leg. 'Your costumes are in there,' he continued, and he pointed at a shabby-looking door with a piece of paper stuck on it on which someone had written DRESING RuM. Inside, there was a smell of must and stale sweat. Marcie looked at the Velcro costumes that were hanging on a rail. She wrinkled her nose.

'This place is horrible, Marcie. Do we have to do this?' I asked. 'Can't you say you're not feeling well?'

Marcie hesitated. 'Er . . . yes. Sam, my love, this is going too far. There are some things that I will do for love but putting on a smelly old Velcro outfit in this stinky dark hole of a place is asking too much and not my idea of fun.'

'I agree,' I said. 'I can't believe he would put you through this.'

Feeling hugely relieved, I followed her back into the hall, where to our surprise I saw Nessa and Uri had arrived. They were handing over what looked like a huge wad of cash to Don, who was looking gleeful.

Nessa saw us and waved us over.

'I'll be off then. These idiot . . . I mean these folks will show you the ropes,' said Don and with a yellow grin at us, he limped off.

I introduced Marcie to Uri.

'Kitted out for the part, I see,' I said. Uri was dressed in an electric blue jumpsuit with black flashes up the sides and his white-blond hair was spiked up like he had a ton of gel on it. Nessa had a pale pink tracksuit on that looked like it might be made of Velcro.

Uri grinned. 'Something like that. You've come for the Velcro experience I assume, Marcie?'

'Yes, but we're not sure, I mean, maybe another day. We were just about to leave, in fact.'

'First time, huh?' asked Uri.

We both nodded.

'Well, you've come all this way – at least give it one try,' he said. 'You'll have a blast. Now let me see if I can get my lights happening.' He picked up a box, went to the wall and plugged in what looked like a slide projector. Immediately the room was flooded with lights, and not just any lights – it was a laser show with swirling lightning flashes, stars and fireworks. It transformed the place, and it no longer looked as spooky as it had done only minutes earlier.

'Over 'ere girls,' said Nessa, and out of a bag that she had brought with her she produced two pale pink tracksuits like the one she was wearing. 'Pure Velcro,' she said as she held them up to us. 'I've been research- in' the material and it needn't be ucky. If you go for the Velcro option you can decide on the design details and so on at a later date.' I took one and the material felt soft and it smelt lovely like it had been washed and hung out to dry in the fresh air.

'Shall we, Marcie? At least give it a go?' I asked.

She glanced up at the trampoline and then at me, then she grinned and I got a glimpse of the old fun Marcie. 'Why not?'

We slipped into the DRESING RuM, and as I was ready first I went out to join Uri.

'Wow! What happened?' I asked. The light show had been turned off and Nessa was busy mopping. I had only been gone about five minutes but the space looked immaculate as if it had been given a lick of paint, not just a wipe over. What's more it smelt divine, of fresh flowers. 'Wow, Nessa!' I said. 'It's as if you waved a magic wand. How did you do it so fast?'

Nessa smiled and tapped the side of her nose. 'Maybe I can work a bit of magic 'ere and there when it's needed. I 'ate a messy room, don't you? I like everythin' to be beautiful and 'armonious. I get upset otherwise.'

'Yes, me too, but how did you do it?' I asked. I took a long look at her and a mad thought occurred to me.

Maybe she was an angel or a fairy godmother. Maybe she really *was* able to do magic.

'I can move fast when I need to as well,' she said, then she turned and went over towards the trampoline. 'Now let me up on that. Give me five minutes to 'ave a dust then up you come.' She started to climb up and Uri came to join me.

'So how's the Zodiac time going?' he asked. 'Second week in, isn't it? Nessa said you missed our help the first week but that wasn't surprising seeing as Mercury was retrograde.'

'Mercury – that's Hermie's business, isn't it?'

'Not his business. Hermie *is* Mercury.'

I felt confused. 'And retrograde – that means going backwards, doesn't it?'

Uri nodded.

'What, like skating backwards?'

Uri laughed. 'No. When Mercury is retrograde, and that happens a few times a year, it means that all sorts of things can go wrong to do with communications.'

'My teacher confiscated my phone.'

'A perfect example. Shame it fell in your Zodiac month.'

Sometimes I found the people in the Celestial Weddings company had a strange way of communicating. Planets, retrograde, zodiacs – why couldn't they just say what they meant? I decided to try and put it in plain language for him.

'I know that the promotion is for a month and Nessa has given me some good advice. She said to let go and enjoy this week and that's what I'm trying to do.'

'That *is* good advice. In fact, the only way to do it. Go with the flow – that's another way of saying it.'

'It was hard to feel enthusiastic when we got here earlier and saw what a dump this was. I can't imagine why you'd want to add Velcro weddings to your list of options. And there's a whole load of other names in my Zodiac phone address book. Where do they come into it? Are they all in the same business?'

Uri sprang back and did a cartwheel across the warehouse floor, then somersaulted back. 'The others will introduce themselves but only if they're prevalent in your chart this month. Not every Zodiac Girl meets all ten of us.'

'Why are *you* in the wedding business, Uri?'

'For you. We adapt ourselves to the needs of who-ever our Zodiac Girl is.'

I felt that he was talking in riddles but then it didn't surprise me – he looked like the sort of person who would do that.

'OK. For me, huh?'

Uri nodded. 'Ten planets. Each sign has a ruling planet.'

Here he goes again, I thought. 'I know, and Venus rules Libra, but I thought there were twelve birth signs, so why only ten ruling planets?' I was sure I'd read it in one of my mags.

Uri nodded. 'Libra and Taurus share Venus as their ruling planet. And Gemini and Virgo share Mercury as theirs. All the others have their own. Aries is ruled by Mars, Cancer by the Moon, Leo by the Sun, Pisces by Neptune, Capricorn by Saturn, Scorpio by Pluto, Sagittarius by Jupiter, Aquarius by Uranus.'

I decided to try and talk to Uri in his own strange language. 'Uri, I hate to say this but . . . I think you might be retrograde because . . . don't be offended, but I think you have a problem with the way you communicate. You need to speak more directly.'

Uri burst out laughing like I'd made the best joke ever.

'What's so funny?' I asked.

'You are,' he replied. 'Each Zodiac Girl makes sense of what's happening to her in her own individual way but . . . I have never come across anyone like you before. You . . . you're amazing. A one-off.'

'Thanks,' I said, although I wasn't sure if he was paying me a compliment or not. *This is a lesson in life*, I decided. *Sometimes I won't have a clue what some people are on about. And that's OK.* 'Now try again, Uri. Try again to explain about you and the wedding business, but try to keep it simple.'

Uri looked as if he might start laughing again. 'OK. So where was I? Right. Uranus is the planet of rebellion, some people say the planet of eccentricity, certainly the unexpected – so my part in the wedding scene is anything that is off the beaten track, like this Velcro wedding. If you'd looked in your chart, you would have seen that Uranus has a strong influence at this time, hence me telling you to expect the unexpected.'

'It's been that all right. First Marcie's list and now this, but I don't understand any of it. I thought I was a Libran and that's ruled by Venus but now you're saying Uranus is an influence?'

'All the planets have some influence on a person's chart at some time or other depending on when you were born. Have you looked at the horoscope that I gave you?'

'Um, not really. That is, I did have a quick look but it looked like a graph. A circle with a load of lines through it. I didn't know what to make of it.'

'Have another look when you get home and you'll see that all the planets are on there. Or don't look. It doesn't really matter. It's what you do with your month that matters.'

'You're talking in riddles again, Uri.'

'OK. In simple language. Once a month, every month somewhere on the planet, one girl is chosen to be a Zodiac Girl. What this means is that she gets the help of the ten planets, who are here on earth in human form. What she does with this help is up to her. It usually happens when the girl is at some kind of turning point in her life.'

'Why can't you just say – once a month, we at Celestial Weddings pick someone to receive our special promotion? The offer only lasts a month – you can repeat that bit if you want because it seems to be important to you. There are ten of us in the business and we will be there to help. There. That's it. Simple. You don't need to mess it up with talking about astrology and stuff because some people aren't into that and you may lose customers.'

Uri's eyes were glistening and I wondered if I'd gone too far and upset him. Then I realized that his face had a strange expression because he was trying not to laugh. Shame, because I liked him even though he was a bit odd and had only been trying to help.

'OK, Chloe,' he said after he'd got his face straight. 'Just go with the flow, Zodiac Girl, and be open to what you can learn. Do what Librans do best and see both sides.'

'Hermie said that too,' I said, and Uri continued

saying something more about being a Zodiac Girl but I wasn't really listening any more though because Marcie came out in her suit. She looked really pretty with her hair pulled up at the back.

'Ready?' she asked.

I nodded.

'OK, we can do it one of two ways,' said Uri. 'The wedding suits are made of Velcro so after the ceremony, when the vicar says, "I now pronounce you man and wife," the bride and groom simply hurl themselves at each other and splat, they are as one. Joined from tip to toe in Holy Matrimony. And Velcro.'

Marcie giggled. 'Sam will love it.'

Mad, I thought, but I didn't say anything because today was just for having fun, not for making serious decisions, and I also knew that there were several options left on Marcie's list after this.

'Come on, Chloe,' said Uri. 'Let's show your sister how it's done. Let's stand side by side and when I say jump, let's jump towards each other.' He clapped his hands, we jumped, and our suits welded together. It was hysterical because he was over six foot and I am only five foot four, so I was stuck to his side. 'Joined at the hip,' I said as he walked off down the room with me firmly clasped to him. 'Isn't that what they say about some married couples?'

Uri laughed.

'What's the second way of doing it?' asked Marcie.

Uri indicated a ladder that led up on to the trampoline. 'For the more adventurous,' he said. He climbed up and held out a hand to me. I clambered on after him and smiled at Nessa, who was still up there. Trampolining was something that I could do. Demi had one in her back garden and we used to go on it every Saturday when we were younger. Nessa winked and gave us the thumbs up.

'OK,' said Uri. 'Imagine that I'm the groom.' He began to jump up and down, up and down, and then he hurled himself against the wall, flinging out his arms and legs as he did so. And there he stayed, suspended halfway up the wall. 'See, the wall is made of Velcro too. Come on, Nessa.'

Nessa bounced and threw herself and there she was, splatted beside him. 'Have a go, Chloe,' she said. 'Come on, Marcie – join in.'

I jumped and jumped, splayed my arms out and went for the wall, where I stuck like glue. 'Come on, Marcie,' I called.

She tentatively began to jump.

'Aim for the wall after your next spring,' said Uri. 'You don't have to be good at trampolining. It's just there to give you a launching pad on to the Velcro.'

Marcie began to bounce, then she flung herself at

the wall. When she realized that she was safe and not going to fall off, she smiled a little. 'And how do you get down?' she asked.

'Easy,' he replied. 'I'll show you.'

I looked over at Uri and the situation suddenly struck me as really funny. The four of us hanging half-way up a wall, having a conversation like it was totally normal. *Once again, not the typical wedding scenario*, I thought, but I was beginning to see that it could be fun and that I had been too closed to Marcie's suggestions in the beginning.

'Exactly,' said Uri as if picking up on my thoughts once again. 'See, getting married can sometimes turn into an intense occasion and the two people who are supposed to be enjoying it the most end up being miserable and stressed. The Velcro experience brings an element of the unexpected into it all. Why go for the boring old convention? Be a rebel on your wedding day, surprise your guests – that's what I say. Live a little, have fun. And in answer to your question, Marcie, to get down you simply peel yourself away, limb by limb.' He peeled away his right arm, then his left, his right leg, then his left, then he leaned forward and peeled his spine away, then leaped back on to the trampoline.

There was no stopping me after that. I bounced with Uri and Nessa. We tried splaying on the wall with our arms and legs in different positions. Marcie had a few tries but she didn't seem to be enjoying it as much as Uri, Nessa and me. Uri was amazing at it. He could do a somersault in the air and land upside down. 'Tadah!' he said with a grin after one amazing leap.

'Wow! Now that would be impressive. If Sam could do that! Don't you think, Marcie?' I said.

'Maybe,' she said. She had a pensive look on her face. 'I'll have to think about it. Might be a bit difficult for doing the toast though, or cutting the cake.'

'We could find a way,' I said. 'This gets my vote.'

Marcie didn't say anything. We climbed down from the trampoline and I took her aside. 'You OK?'

'I'm not sure this is for me,' she said and her bottom lip wobbled a little. 'I mean, imagine the wedding photos.'

'But Nessa said she can make something lovely,' I said.

'In Velcro! You've changed your tune,' said Marcie. 'What's the matter with you? I thought you wanted the best for me. Silk and lace and tiny mother-of-pearl beads.'

'I . . . I . . . Marcie, it's *your* list. I'm trying to be help-ful.' I decided to quote what Nessa had said. 'I am trying to see both sides, be easy-going. Nessa says—'

Marcie wasn't appeased. 'Nessa this, Nessa that. You've only just met her.'

'I know, but honest, Marcie, if you'd seen her gorgeous designs at the wedding show and met her colleagues, you'd be impressed too. And I won some kind of astrology thing where I get her advice for a month. And she does talk sense.'

'You've just fallen under her spell because she's so beautiful. And you're not the only one who knows about astrology, you know. I had a flatmate when I was at college who was Libran and there's another trait I remember about them. Easily influenced. And that's you. Adamant about one thing one week and then someone comes along and turns your head.'

'Hey! That's so not fair,' I said. 'I . . . I . . .'

'Yeah. You hate me. Go on, say it. Be the princess who didn't get her way.'

What on earth is going on? I asked myself. *Planning a wedding is supposed to be such a happy thing to do but this is turning weird. I don't seem to be able to do anything right. I resist Marcie's plans and she says I'm selfish. I go along with them and try and get into it and she accuses me of being easily influenced. I can't win!* I decided to shut up and not say another word. After I'd changed back into my jeans and T-shirt we said goodbye to Uri and Nessa, then we drove home. It was a silent trip, both of us wearing sulky expressions, me with my arms firmly crossed over my chest. I glanced over at Marcie. *It's you who's acting the spoilt princess blaming everyone else for Sam's stupid list*, I thought, as I mentally struck number two from the list.

'Sam ought to be here with you doing this,' I said. I'm just your sister. It's not my fault you aren't enjoying this.'

'Don't I know it,' she said through gritted teeth. 'Sam is probably sitting in a country pub somewhere having the time of his life. The way I feel at the moment, I think I'd like to kill him rather than marry him.'

Oops! I thought.

Chapter Eight

Options Schmoptions

'So, Chloe, any more ideas about what you want to do when you leave school?' asked my sister Jane as she forked her way through Mum's casserole, picking out the mushrooms.

Oh God, not this again! I thought. 'I might become a trampoline artist in the circus,' I replied. 'Or maybe a window cleaner. I can't decide.' I thought I was being quite funny but nobody laughed.

Jane rolled her eyes.

'Marcie was right about you being easily influenced, you know,' said Clare, my other sister. 'Not because you're a Libran – we all know that astrology is a load of baloney – but because you just are, always have been.'

'Duh! I was joking,' I protested. It was the evening after Marcie and I had been to the Incredible Velcro place and my sisters were round for supper. Sadly, what should have been a nice girlie time with us discussing Marcie's wedding and what we were going to wear was fast turning into a character assassination of the worst kind, that character being me. I looked at each of them in turn. Even if you didn't know them, you would know that they were sisters. Like Marcie, Jane and Clare also take after my mum and have her chestnut brown hair, her brown eyes, fine features and slightly small mouth. I'm the only blonde of the girls in our family and the only one with a dimple, right in the middle of my chin. I take after Dad, who was fair when he had hair but was pretty well bald last time I saw him. I wonder sometimes if they are mean to me because I look like him and they don't want to be reminded.

'Gullible is the word I'd use,' said Clare.

'Always changing her mind, it's true,' said Mum.

'That's not a bad thing,' I protested. 'There are two sides to every story and surely you Clare, as a lawyer, ought to know that.'

She raised her eyebrows and fixed me with a stern look. 'Only one side that wins though.'

'OK, if I am easily influenced then what about Marcie? Before she met Sam Hunkalunk, she wanted a normal wedding in a beautiful dress with a fabulous reception. Instead, we're on some kind of weird adventure week.' As I said the words though, I remembered what Nessa and Uri had said about not settling for convention and the fun of being a rebel and doing something wacky. Despite my first choice still being the traditional wedding, I wasn't as one hundred per cent against Sam's list as I had been in the beginning. The alternatives didn't have to be tacky. With the right organization and Nessa to help, they could possibly be made to work. 'I'm trying to be open-minded, and that's more than you lot are about astrology. It's actually very scientific.'

Jane grinned. 'You know, you could make a good lawyer, Chloe. You do know how to argue.'

'Pff!' I said.

Clare laughed. 'Pff? Yes, very articulate for a wannabe lawyer.'

'I'm not a wannabe lawyer,' I protested. 'I'm a wannabe don't know what I wannabe.' Through all the banter, I noticed that Marcie was quiet and I wondered if she was still cross with me for enthusing about the Velcro idea and the roller skating. 'You OK, Marcie?'

She gave an unconvincing nod.

'She's having wedding nerves, aren't you, love?' asked Mum.

Marcie shrugged. 'Not sure what I'm having. Not sure I'll even be having a wedding. I mean, maybe we should just skip that part and do what you did, Jane, with your Michael – just live together. Maybe

Sam was right – who needs a wedding in this day and age?'

I could not believe my ears! *First she shatters my dreams by saying she doesn't want a conventional wedding, and I've been doing my best to get over that and be easy-going. I've tried to compromise and go along with the plan and now she's thinking about giving up on that too.* I looked over at my sisters and wondered if I might be adopted. I watched them sitting there with their neat features to match their neat clothes. Jane and Clare like to wear navy a lot – smart suits and smart shoes to go with their smart lives. I like pink and pretty pastel colours and make-up and dressing up. Jane and Clare used to share a room when they lived here many years ago and even that was neat, painted a soft grey and loaded with books, not fun books but books about facts. I used to share a room with Marcie but as soon as Jane and Clare went, I got their old room at the back of the house and the first thing I did was paint it baby pink and put up my wedding posters. They were *horrified.* I used to think Marcie and I were a bit alike but the older she gets, the more like the others she becomes, so yes, adopted. Maybe. No, not maybe. I must be. Definitely. *I wish someone like Nessa was my real mother,* I thought. *Someone with a sense of style who likes beautiful things in life and seems to get what I'm about.*

'I despair. I am going up to my room and I don't want to talk to anyone, OK?' I said.

Clare shrugged, Jane continued picking out her mushrooms, Marcie stared out of the window with a moody expression on her face and Mum just smiled. 'Don't forget to look over any homework you've been given for the half term,' she said as though she hadn't even noticed that my sisters had been picking on me.

I went up and sat on the window ledge and stared out into the dark. *I don't know where I fit in this life,* I thought. *On the one hand, I know exactly who I am, Chloe Bradbury. I live at 23, Midhurst Street, I know I am the youngest of four girls and I go to school. On the other hand, I have no idea who I am or what I am meant to do but it didn't seem to matter until now. Why can't I just be me? A schoolgirl? That's my career for now.* I spent another few minutes thinking about job options. *Fashion maybe. I like clothes and design. Or maybe travel? I am good at languages. I could do tours or translating. But maybe I'd miss home. Maybe I should stay here and . . . open a shop. I have a good eye. I could make it look beautiful.* I wrote down my various options, then sighed. Mum and my sisters were right – I did keep changing my mind. I needed something to cheer myself up so I got down from the ledge and went to the carrier bag in my wardrobe with all my wedding stuff in it. Looking through the glossy pages always gave me a lift but this time, as I flicked through and stared at the beautiful dresses and the wonderful locations, none of the gloss rubbed off on me. My sure-fire method to make myself feel better was failing me and I felt flat. Maybe happy wedding days happened to other people, not to me or Marcie or anyone else in the Bradbury family.

Chapter Nine

The Madness Continues

Call Nessa, said a voice in my head as I waited in our front room for Demi, Maryam and Marcie to arrive the next day. I had been reading over my horoscope and thinking about what it all meant. *She said she's here to help. Special offer, one month only.* I pressed the button next to her name and she picked up immediately.

''Ello, darlin'.'

'Nessa, heeeelp! I have been trying your way of doing things and it doesn't seem to be working out and now Marcie is crosser than ever with me. What should I do?'

'Tough it out, doll. You 'ave to give it a bit longer,' she said. 'I know you might be losin' patience a bit and that would be because you 'ave Aries risin'—'

'Aries rising? I thought I was a Libran. What do you mean, I have Aries rising?'

'Everyone's Sun sign changes every month accordin' to the date that they are born so everyone born on

23rd September to 22nd October is born under the Sun sign of Libra, yeah?'

'Yes.'

''Ave you never wondered why you're not all the same then? All the Librans you know? You'll 'ave some similar traits but you'll all be individuals and that's because there are other planets and factors that affect your 'oroscope and one of them is your risin' sign.'

'So what's that then? Isn't that Libra too?'

'No. Sun signs changes every month but a risin' sign changes every two hours, which is why different people born on the same day will be different – because although, say, they are all born on 28th September, they won't all be born at four o'clock in the mornin'. Some will be born at six, others at eight and so on, and so they will all have different risin' signs.'

'Right. I remember Uri saying something like that. I've been reading over my chart too and trying to understand that. It's quite complicated, isn't it?'

'Don't worry, Chloe, it takes a while to sink in. Like you – you were born at six in the evenin', the risin' sign at that time is Aries, at eight o'clock it changes to Taurus and at ten o'clock it changes to Gemini and so on, through all the signs.'

'And that makes everyone individual unless of

course you are born at the same time, at the same hour in the same place as someone.'

'Exactly. You're a bright kid. Your Sun sign determines your general characteristics – how you look, how you are on a superficial level – but your risin' sign also contributes to makin' up your personality and you have Aries risin', which will sometimes make you impetuous and impatient. People who have a strong Aries in their charts tend to be leaders and have lots of energy, but they do tend to rush at things.'

'I think I understand,' I said.

'Just be patient, go through the list with Marcie, let all the cards be out on the table before you say what you think should or shouldn't 'appen.'

'OK. You're saying that I have to slow down. I think I can do that,' I said. 'Already the first two options on the list didn't turn out how I thought.' Nessa put things so nicely that it all seemed do-able and I felt OK, unlike when my family spoke to me, when it always seemed that I was doing something wrong. 'So will I see you today?'

'Not me but you'll see Uri.'

'Great,' I said. I liked Uri. 'Got to go – I can see Marcie's car pulling up.'

''Ave a good day then. Laters, Zodiac Girl.'

'Laters, Nessa.' Talking to her had made me feel a million times better and I went to open the door for

Marcie feeling optimistic about trying out another option on the list.

'What's up with Marcie?' whispered Demi as we squeezed into the back of her car after everyone had arrived.

I shrugged. 'Marcie, what's up?'

'Nothing. I'm fine,' she said unconvincingly.

Maryam grimaced at me and Demi and I nodded. Fine she definitely wasn't. I decided to try and cheer her up by being mega cooperative.

'Hey, it's bungee jumping today, isn't it, Marcie? Should be a laugh.'

'Maybe,' she replied in a gloomy tone, 'but I might skip it. We'll see.'

Amazing, I thought. *Nessa was so right about everything. I am hardly having to object at all because Marcie seems to be talking herself out of all the options on her own without me making a scene.*

'We should at least see what's involved,' I said. It was a lesson for life, I decided – go with the flow, keep an open mind, and watch how everything changes including how people feel about things.

The Bungee Bride branch of Celestial Weddings was situated on the ground floor of a tall office block on the outskirts of Osbury.

Uri appeared from the back room when we went inside.

'You again,' I said with a smile.

'Yes,' he replied. 'I told you I did the wackiest weddings.' He gave me a wink. 'Good to see you again and glad you're up to try another alternative. Impressive.'

'Nuh,' mumbled Marcie, who still didn't look happy at all.

Uri handed us a bungee brochure that showed all the things you could throw yourself off.

'Can you think of a better way to seal the deal,' he continued, 'than by jumping off the nearest bridge or high building, arms entwined with your loved one?'

I glanced up from the 'interesting' locations from which you could throw yourself into oblivion. 'Duh, yeah!' I said. 'But I am trying to remain open-minded until we have been through the whole list.'

Demi had gone white. 'Please, *please*, Marcie. Please don't make us do this. I didn't realize it was bungee jumping today and I want to be a mate but I hate heights. I'll be sick.'

And get whiplash, I thought. I decided that now would be the time to share my 'path of least resistance' attitude to life.

'Chill,' I said. 'It'll be fun!'

'I won't make *you* do it,' said Marcie. 'All you and

Chloe and Maryam have to do is be bridesmaids and look pretty.'

I gave Demi a smug look. I was right. It would be fine.

'It's Sam and I who have to make the jump,' she added.

I wanted to ask her if she'd gone completely insane, but I was beginning to think that maybe she had. Maybe this was what love did to you. Turned you into a total nut job. I handed her the brochure.

She took it and glanced down the options. 'OK. A challenge. We don't have to decide anything yet, do we?'

Uri shook his head. 'No. I'll show you how it's done. Now follow me, girls.'

He led us out of his office into the hall, where we took a lift up to the twentieth floor. Up top, it was cold and breezy and all of us pulled our coats tighter around us to keep out the wind. On the corner of the flat roof was a crane that went up and up into the sky. Marcie looked at it and gulped. I took her hand. *She ought to be backing out about now,* I thought but she took a step towards the crane.

'You don't have to do this,' I said.

'I do,' she said in an unhappy voice. 'Sam called last night to see how it was going. He's so sorry he can't be here and said I have to be his ears and eyes in this. He calls every night and loves hearing about what we're doing. I can't back out now.'

Uri ushered us on to a platform with low walls. *Duh? Path of least resistance? This isn't supposed to be happening*, I thought. Uri closed the gate, pressed the control buttons and we were swung up and into the sky.

'Warghhhhh!' Marcie, Maryam, Demi and I screeched as one. We reached for each other's hands and clung on to each other.

'It's perfectly safe,' he beamed and he swung us up higher. I dared a peek. The ground below appeared further and further away. 'Arggghhh!'

'This is the typical height that people jump from,' said Uri. 'Look, Chloe, you can see for miles in every direction. Look around, breathe it in.'

I had my eyes shut tight. 'No. No way. Marcie, this is mad. Sam should be doing this. It's not fair that he's not the one doing this so that he can see for himself how scary it is. I don't care about not resisting. I hate this. It's insane. Please. Enough. Marcie. Uri. Please let's go back now.'

I opened my eyes to look at her pleadingly. She took a peep over the edge. 'Er . . . yes,' she said as she stepped back from the edge. 'C-can we go down now, Uri?'

'You're the boss,' he said. 'It's your wedding.'

'No she isn't,' I said. 'Sam's the boss. It's *his* wedding.' I couldn't help it. It was out before I could bite my tongue. I felt the platform lurch and my stomach clench with fear. I so hoped that it was safe.

Moments later, the movement stopped. 'You can open your eyes now, girls,' said Uri. 'We're back on the roof.'

We opened our eyes and I took a deep breath of relief.

'So that gives you some idea of how it might feel. Exhilarating, huh?' said Uri. 'And you choose the location. We can do it from most high buildings or a bridge or a canyon, whatever you prefer.'

'I think I'd prefer a cup of tea on level ground,' said Marcie. Maryam, Demi and I nodded back at her.

'There's also our parachute dive wedding. It's going to be very popular. Would madam like to see a video?' Uri called after us as he opened the gate for us and we headed for the door that led to the lift. 'Or maybe you'd like to hear about our paragliding? That's a super option. You can do it together while your guests watch from the cliff edge. It's beautifully symbolic – a couple stepping over the edge, going into the unknown.' For a moment, Uri looked dreamy and I wondered if he'd ever been in love. In the meantime, Demi looked like she was going to throw up.

'That was truly *horrible*,' she groaned, 'and we didn't even jump. Remind me again why we're doing this.'

'For Sam,' said Marcie in a clipped voice. 'He wants the day to be fun.'

'Fun yes, terrifying no. Isn't the fact that you're marrying him enough?' I asked. 'Won't *that* make the day fun?'

Marcie shrugged. 'It ought to, oughtn't it? I don't know. I want to make him happy. And marriage is a partnership. I have to give his suggestions a chance.'

'You want to make him happy, but what about you, Marcie? I can honestly say I've never seen you more unhappy than this week,' I said and Demi and Maryam nodded in agreement. I knew that I was going back on everything that Nessa had advised but she hadn't been up there, miles above the ground.

A flash of irritation crossed Marcie's face. 'Well, nothing is decided,' she said in a clipped tone, 'and we still have a few more to try,' but with a shaky hand, she ran a pencil through option three.

We went back to our house later that day and when Marcie had gone after a cup of tea with Mum, Demi, Maryam and I flicked through our Bridesmaids' album in great sadness as though someone in it had died.

'We have to face it,' I said. 'We have to let go of

what we want. It has to be *her* dream wedding, not ours.'

'Yes,' said Demi and Maryam.

I picked up my Zodiac phone which was bleeping that I had a message. **Let's not be rigid in our thinking,** from Dr Cronus, aka Saturn. I read it out to the girls.

'Whatever,' said Demi.

'I guess,' said Maryam. 'We haven't met Dr Cronus, have we?'

I shook my head. 'No, and I don't think he was at the wedding show either.'

The Zodiac phone bleeped again. This time it said, **Life is determined not by what happens but how you respond to what happens,** from Dr Cronus again. I read it out in my poshest voice and Demi and Maryam cracked up.

'Well, I would have thrown up if we'd stayed up on that crane,' said Maryam. 'That's how I would have responded.'

'Me too,' said Demi.

'But we're agreed,' I said. 'We'll go along with the list with no objections until she decides?'

'And then can we object?' asked Demi.

'Um, not sure,' I said. 'Her wedding, not ours.'

'We'll put our own desires aside for Marcie's happiness,' said Demi.

'Even if it means madness,' said Maryam.

'I suppose,' I said in a hushed voice. 'That will be my motto from now on. Her wedding, not mine.'

As we sat looking through my album, I realized that I had to let go of agonizing about how it could have been if we had done it my way. Poor Marcie. It *was* her wedding and I had been insensitive by not really listening to what she wanted. *I know she's trying to please Sam*, I thought, *and maybe that's enough, but . . . I wonder what she really wants in her heart.*

Chapter Ten

Underwater Bride

Thursday was number four on the list – the Aquarium wedding. Marcie, Maryam, Demi and I were sitting snug as bugs in the Europa cafe in Osbury, sipping mugs of hot chocolate before we went to the Aquarium. It was raining so hard outside that we could have had an underwater wedding in the street, so we weren't in any hurry to get going.

Marcie had the brochure on the table in front of her. 'Sam, the vicar and I swim in a giant fish tank,' she explained. 'You girls wear wetsuits, flippers and goggles with bits of seaweed ribbon strewn in your hair. The rest of the guests watch from outside the tank. For music, we could have the sound of whales or dolphins honking in the distance.'

'And no doubt it would be seafood at the reception?' Demi asked innocently.

Marcie nodded. 'Yes. I think that's the idea.'

'Maybe you and Sam could jump out of the tank when it's time for wedding cake – you know, like feeding time for the dolphins at Sea World,' said Maryam equally innocently.

'Ohmicod!' said Demi. 'At least the photos will be different. No one will have wedding pics to top us in wetsuit gear.'

I knew that they were having a laugh at Marcie's expense and I couldn't blame them. All her wedding guests would laugh too if she didn't come to her senses soon. In the meantime though, I had sworn to myself that I would be supportive to the very last option on the list. 'I'm sure Nessa could make you something gorgeous, Marcie. A dinky little swimsuit in white with some lovely freshwater pearls sewn in. It might actually look really lovely, the two of you swimming, your hair flowing out behind you.'

'You seem to have forgotten that I can't put my head under the water, never mind *swim* under water,' sighed Marcie. 'It seems to have slipped Sam's mind too although he would probably say anything is possible if you have the right attitude, then arrange for me to have diving lessons before the wedding.'

I had forgotten. Marcie can swim but she's never liked it. Some stupid boy dunked her head under when she was in junior school and she gets panicky in the water. Maybe Sam didn't know how much it freaked her out, but then maybe she hadn't let on. It seemed that she wanted to please him so much that she didn't always tell him what she was feeling about things.

'So are we going to go along for a demo or not?' I asked. I wondered if Nessa would show up with one of her planet colleagues. I had noticed on my Zodiac phone that one of them was called Captain John Dory – aka Neptune. Neptune was the king of the sea so, out of all of Nessa's colleagues, he was the one I'd expected to see today.

'Demo?' asked Marcie. '*Demo?* I'll give that Sam Hendy a demo he won't forget in a hurry when he gets back.' The sharpness in her voice took me by surprise. She very deliberately got out a pen from her bag and with a dramatic flourish, she crossed out number four on the list. 'There. That's what I think of your aquarium wedding, Sam Hendy. You can take your wedding list and shove it—'

An old lady on the next table glanced up.

'Marcie,' I warned before she said anything embarrassing. 'We're in public.' Part of me was glad that Marcie was at last seeing sense, but I do hate it when people make a scene.

Marcie clocked the old dear and rolled her eyes. 'Sorry. I got engaged to the world's greatest IDIOT and I've only just realized!'

'Lucky you,' said the lady. 'Better to realize now than in twenty years when it's too late.'

'Exactly!' said Marcie. 'Now then, who's for a big piece of that chocolate fudge cake I saw at the counter before? It's about time us girls had some real fun!'

Now what's happening? I wondered as she got up and ordered four huge pieces of cake. As she stood at the counter, my Zodiac phone bleeped that I had a message from Nessa. **An encounter with Pluto means transformation,** it said. I was about to text back and ask what she meant when Marcie reappeared with our fudge cake.

'When the going gets tough, the tough eat chocolate cake,' she said.

'Good plan,' said Demi.

'Best one yet,' said Maryam and as we all tucked in, I thought that the main transformation was going to be on our waistlines.

'Sam can't accuse me of not trying out everything,' said Marcie when later the same day she parked outside Jungle Jamboree, a shop that had gorilla costumes in the window. After our cakes had been eaten and the rain had ceased, Marcie had insisted that we try out the last option on the list.

'She is joking, isn't she?' whispered Demi as we got out and followed her into the shop.

'I think so,' I said. 'I'm not sure.' I glanced at Marcie. Something had happened this morning and she had a determined expression on her face – like she'd made up her mind about something and there was no going back.

'Option number five, the Bridezilla wedding,' Marcie pronounced once we got inside to find an empty shop. She dinged a bell on the counter to alert whoever owned the place that they had customers. 'The idea is that Sam and I wear gorilla outfits. You girls would be chimps.'

'Are you serious?' asked Demi.

'I'm not but Sam was, and how *ridiculous* is that?' said Marcie. 'But as we're here, we may as well explore all the fancy dress options so that when I report back, he knows that I did the job thoroughly and he can't blame me for . . . well, for what I've decided.' There was something in her tone that made me think that Sam was in for a telling off. A big telling off.

A few moments later, an extraordinary looking man came out of the back. He was tall and pale and looked every inch a Goth prince – he was dressed in a purple velvet suit with dark hair tied back in a ponytail. He gave us a small bow.

'Hello, ladeez, and how can I be of help?' he asked in an accent that I couldn't quite place – maybe Russian?

'Great Dracula costume,' Demi said.

The man looked affronted. 'Dracula? But zis iz not ze fancy clothes. Zis is how I am normally dressing.'

Demi grinned. 'And you have a great accent too.'

The man bowed again. 'PJ's ze name, transformation ze game.' He indicated the rows and rows of costumes

'Ah. You're Pluto, aren't you?' I asked. 'Nessa said we might see you.'

'And you must be ze Zodiac Girl, yah?'

I smiled. 'Chloe's ze name –'

'Being bonkers ze game,' Demi joined in.

'Do you know this man?' asked Marcie.

I shook my head. 'No, but he's in the wedding business with Nessa, right?'

'I am in ze business of change, transformation, like a caterpillar to ze butterfly and yes, for zis month, we iz doing the wedding. Other times I do interior design or makeovers.'

'Fab,' said Demi.

'We're here to look at the gorilla costumes,' said Marcie. 'For my wedding.'

PJ smiled. 'Now zat I can help with,' he said and pointed us in the direction of a rack of furry costumes at the back of the shop. 'Ze Bridezilla wedding iz very popular. Help yourselves to anyzing else you vould like to be trying,' he said. 'I 'ave some jobs to do while you iz dressing.' He fluttered his hands at us as if to say that we should get on with the business of dressing up.

Dutifully, we looked through the rack, found our sizes, then went to put our monkey costumes on.

Demi and I were ready first. We looked at each other and burst out laughing. We stood in front of the mirror while we waited for Marcie. We looked totally silly.

'Not exactly what I had in mind for my first brides-maid outfit,' I said as I did a twirl.

'I know it's not,' said Demi. 'You're taking this very well, Chloe. For someone who wanted to dress in silk and lace.'

'It's not over yet,' I said. 'If I thought this madness was going to happen for real, I think I would be freaked out of my mind but Nessa has been so brilliant – telling me to chill and see what happens – and you know what? If I am honest, it has been a fun week.'

'And it looks like you won't have to do a crazy wedding in the end,' said Demi. 'After this morning, I think Marcie has finally seen sense.'

'Maybe,' I said. 'Nessa was so right. She said that if I didn't resist it would be OK, and it does seem that has happened. Like she's come to the conclusion by herself that this isn't her dream wedding. It's weird, isn't it? Like we've both changed our minds. She thinks the list is bonkers now and I actually think some of the options have potential.'

We high-fived each other just as Maryam came out of the changing room. She made a noise like a chimp and immediately Demi and I joined in and started aping around doing funny monkey walks and noises and having a great laugh, although it was hard to breathe with the costume heads on. PJ didn't seem to mind us messing about. He looked over at us and gave us a thumbs up. Inside, I felt a huge sense of relief about Marcie's turnaround. The Bridezilla option was the one that I had worried about the most. It wasn't dangerous or scary, just funny and different, and it might have appealed to Marcie's sense of mischievousness and love of a practical joke. There had been a distinct possibility that she might go for it before her change in mood today.

'Least we won't have to worry about having our hair done,' laughed Demi as she pretended to try and climb up the dressing room curtains.

'OK, I'm ready, girls,' said Marcie from behind the curtain.

I began to sing the wedding march. 'Dah dah da dah, dah dah da—' I whipped back the curtain of the dressing room and there, moving very slowly as if walking down an aisle, was a large gorilla. A gorilla wearing a white veil and a dinky tiara and carrying a bunch of white roses. We burst out laughing and then Marcie began to lark about with us as if we really were a family of chimps. Demi started to groom me, then I pretended to pick bugs from her fur and eat them, and it wasn't long before we were on the floor laughing.

Demi made us line up so that she could take a group photo on her phone.

'So, what do you think, Marcie?' I asked after Demi had taken her shot.

'Bit hot,' she replied and she pulled the gorilla head off. 'People must be insane to consider this as a wedding option. I mean, apart from the fact that we all look totally stupid, it's roasting in these costumes.'

Maryam, Demi and I did the same. 'Phew!' said Maryam. 'Yeah. It is kind of hard to breathe in there.' We did look flushed from wearing so much fur.

'There are endless possibilities,' said Marcie as she looked around the shop, 'not just gorillas.'

'Go right ahead,' said PJ. 'Try everyzing. Be transforming yourselves!'

'Thanks,' we chorused. *Brill,* I thought. I loved dressing up and there were loads of lovely looking costumes as well as the comedy ones.

Marcie picked through a rack to the front of the shop. 'We could all dress as Superheroes. How about Spiderman?' she asked as she held up a Spiderman outfit. 'Sam could swing in from the building opposite

115

the church. Or we could dress as Batman and Robin. That should make it special.'

I took a long look at her to try and gauge if she was serious. She was still looking flushed from wearing the big monkey head but there was something in her tone that was worrying. I wasn't sure if she was sad about Sam or mad with him.

'Or we could do Victorian or Goth or Vampires or cavemen,' she continued as she held a club up in the air. 'I could bash Sam over the head after I've taken the vows.'

Hmm, maybe mad with him, I thought as she swished the club through the air with some force.

I could have agreed with Marcie about how stupid the fancy dress option was but I was determined not to crack now, having got so far. It looked as if Marcie was working it all out on her own. I picked up a horned helmet. 'Or what about Vikings?' I asked.

'Yeah, brilliant,' said Marcie. 'Or Robin Hood and Maid Marion? Or Star Trek characters?'

'Are you two on drugs?' asked Demi. 'What is going on?'

Another costume caught Marcie's eye and she rushed over, picked out a long white dress and held it up against her. 'A Princess Leia outfit. We could have a Star Wars wedding.' She looked at her reflection holding up the white dress. It was as close to a normal wedding outfit as there was in the shop.

'Ve have ze vedding dresses,' said PJ. 'You iz coming upping ze stairs. All by ze Nessa. She iz up zere making, creating, sewing ze dresses.'

We all looked at each other.

'Wouldn't do any harm to just try,' I said.

'Just a little look,' said Demi.

'It is best to consider all options,' said Maryam.

'And I vill do ze hair and ze make-ups,' said PJ.

Up we went without any persuasion. It was like walking into a fairy grotto with silver, white and mirrored walls, little lights strewn everywhere like at Christmas, and it smelt divine – of tuberose. Rows of beautiful white and cream dresses hung on rails along the walls, with a couple of examples on dummies towards the back of the shop. On a counter to the left were tiaras in mother-of-pearl and diamonds, one of white leaves and another made from what looked like silver leaves, and on the wall to the right were shelves of fabric: silk, satin, velvet. It was wedding heaven. We ooh-ed and aah-ed. I felt like I had found my true home.

'Nessa, ve have ze customers,' said PJ.

We heard a rustle, and a moment later Nessa appeared. She was wearing one of her creations, a sheath in gossamer silk that fell from her shoulders to her feet. Her hair was up and she had on a tiny crown. She was one hundred per cent goddess.

'What do you think?' she asked. 'This is a new dress that I've been working on.'

'Divine,' we chorused.

'Ta,' she said. 'Now then. 'ow can we 'elp? First of all though, PJ, let's 'ave some bubbly for the bride to be, and are you 'ungry? Bring some chocolate for the girls.' She glanced over and winked. 'I do think that planning a wedding needs to be fun on every level, don't you? Let's 'ave some music too.'

PJ disappeared down the stairs while Nessa put some upbeat music on. The next hour went by in a happy blur as each of us tried on the prettiest dresses and quaffed sparkling elderflower while Marcie drank champagne with peach juice. We ate scrumptious chocolates with fudge centres and boogied around to the music. Marcie tried on loads of different outfits and every shoe that Nessa showed her, from stunning high-heeled silver sandals to dinky ballet shoes made from the softest leather. Everything looked good but then Nessa insisted that Marcie try on the new dress that she'd been wearing. She and PJ took her away and left Demi, Maryam and me to continue trying on the accessories and flick through *Brides* magazines.

'This is what it's all about, isn't it?' I said as I popped another chocolate in my mouth and sat back in one of the chairs near the counter. 'Great fabrics, lovely smells, good music. It's a whole experience of loveliness.'

Demi did a spin. 'Loveliness,' she repeated.

Maryam got up to join her then stopped and stared. 'Oh my God!' she said.

Demi and I looked in the direction she was staring. 'Oh my God!' we echoed.

Marcie was standing by the door in Nessa's dress. PJ had done her make-up just perfectly, not too much, just enough to give her face light and a touch of gloss. Her hair was up and Nessa had threaded some pearl beads through the back. Around her neck she had a stunning freshwater pearl choker. My eyes filled with tears. Here was my sister Marcie, the bride. This was how she was meant to look. 'Oh Marcie,' I said. 'You look *beautiful.*'

Marcie stepped forward and looked at herself in the mirror. She caught her breath and her eyes glistened. 'I do, don't I?' she whispered.

Behind her, Nessa and PJ appeared. 'Every inch the beautiful bride,' said Nessa, then she turned and ushered PJ away. 'Let's leave them alone to talk about it,' she said.

As soon as they'd gone, Marcie's eyes filled with the tears she'd been holding back. I went over and put my hand on her arm. 'You all right?' I asked.

She nodded but she didn't looked all right.

'You look so beautiful, Marcie,' said Demi.

She looked at her reflection and nodded.

'Is this what you really want, Marcie? Is this the sort of wedding outfit that you would really like?' I asked.

She sniffed back a tear and nodded. 'I would. I'd like to look beautiful on my day. Not in Velcro or on roller skates or underwater. I just want to look like a bride.'

'Princess for a day,' I said.

Marcie nodded. 'You guys are the best, you know. You've been so brilliant this week and gone along with everything without complaining and you, Chloe . . .' she began to sob, 'you even tried to roller-skate for me.'

'It's your wedding, Marcie,' I said. 'You should have what *you* want. You were right. I was just being selfish in the beginning, trying to make you have my perfect wedding when of course, it's your day.' I really meant it too.

I put my arms round Marcie and she sobbed harder and blubbed into my neck. I let her cry for a while. 'Can I do anything? What is it? What's made you so upset?'

Marcie sighed. 'You. You have, Chloe. The way you've been this week has been amazing and it's shown me, that's what love is, true love. It's giving up what you want to make someone else happy, the way you've done. I know, I know you've had your dream of your day when you get to be bridesmaid ever since you were little and I know how much it's meant to you but you let it all go for me. For me, your big stupid sister with my mad ideas.'

'It's your wedding,' I repeated.

Marcie shook her head. 'Yes. It is. And Sam's, more Sam's wedding. I . . . I've been so busy trying to please him and accommodate what he wanted that I didn't even tell him what I wanted and . . . he didn't ask. Hasn't asked! You were right yesterday. Sam should have been here with me. *He* should have been going through this important time with me, not you guys, and he should have also been asking me what *my* ideas were. I have to have a say too.'

'I'm sure he was going to get round to asking you and he'll be here for the wedding,' I said. 'That's the *most* important time when it comes down to it.'

Marcie shook her head again. 'No. No. I need him now. Or at least I did.'

'What do you mean, you did?' I asked. 'Have you decided to go ahead with a traditional wedding after all?'

'No,' said Marcie. 'I have changed my mind about the list and about the wedding. I know that's usually your thing, Chloe, but this time, it's me. There isn't going to be a wedding, not any more. I'm through with this whole charade. I'll tell Sam tonight. I have decided, the wedding's off.'

Chapter Eleven

Doghouse

'What on earth have you done?' asked Jane when she came over later that night. Clare had arrived over an hour earlier and was in the kitchen with Mum, who was trying to comfort Marcie by making her endless cups of tea.

'Me? *Nothing*,' I replied. Mum had asked the same question just after we'd arrived home and she'd seen Marcie's red eyes. And so had Jane when she'd arrived soon after Mum had called me. It so wasn't fair.

'You must have said something. Mum said that Jane said that Marcie said that you'd said something.'

'Me? No. Honest. I asked her what *she* wanted for her wedding, that's all, and . . . and I might have asked where Sam had been while we'd been doing this wedding research, like it seemed to me that he should have been the one trying out all the mad ideas with her.'

Clare clucked her tongue with disapproval. 'That will be it then.'

'It's not fair to blame me, Clare. I've done every-thing I could to support Marcie even though from the beginning I thought that her wedding ideas were high on the bonkers scale. I didn't see you or Mum or Jane exactly volunteering to go bungee jumping or tram-polining or dressing up as a gorilla and making a berk of yourselves.'

'I had to work but I doubt I'd have done it anyway. In fact, I knew it would all go wrong,' said Clare, 'as soon as I saw that stupid list.'

'So you thought it was mad too?'

'Yes, course, but I never actually thought she was going to take it seriously. I credited her with more of a brain. So the wedding's off, I take it?'

'I think so.'

'Has she told Sam?'

'She called him not long after we left the fancy dress shop.'

'How did he take it?'

'Badly, I think.'

'Where is she?'

I jerked my thumb towards the kitchen and off she went. I couldn't decide what to do or where to go. My head was spinning with choices.

Go into the kitchen with the others? But when Mum wasn't blaming me, Clare was going on about what a let-down men were or Marcie was crying, so the kitchen wasn't a great option.

Stay put? I could stay in the hall and phone Demi or Maryam, who had gone home for their supper. Maybe not. What could they say? Or maybe I should – they're my mates after all and understand the situation better than anyone. But then, maybe they'd had enough of it all.

Bedroom? Should I go upstairs for a cuddle with Sergeant Ted? He was a teddy bear – what could he do? But then cuddling him always made me feel better.

Bathroom? Have a lovely long relaxing bubble bath?

Or should I go back in and see Marcie? Maybe I should run her a bath?

I took a step towards the kitchen. No, that didn't feel right.

I took a step for the stairs. No, I'd feel out of things up there.

Bathroom? No, it would be wrong to lock myself away at a time like this.

Oh God! Decisions, decisions. *WHY CAN I NEVER MAKE UP MY MIND? Things can't possibly get any worse,* I thought, when the phone rang. As there was no movement coming from the kitchen, I picked up. It was Sam.

'Oh!' I gulped. 'Hi. Um . . . Sam. I, er . . . do you want Marcie?'

'No, Chloe, I wanted to talk to you.' He sounded sad.

'Oh well, here I am, yes, it's me,' I said, trying to sound bright and cheerful although that was the last thing I was feeling. 'And how are you?'

'How do you think I am, Chloe? How do you *think* I am?'

Not happy, that's for sure, I thought. *I can tell that much from your voice.* 'Er . . . ooh . . . Are you sure you don't want to talk to Marcie? She is here, in the kitchen.'

'Marcie has made it very clear that she doesn't want to speak to me. Not now. Not ever again. Says I don't know about the true meaning of love. Says you do. Do you, Chloe? Because if you do, maybe you could let me know what it is because it's a mystery to me.'

'Me? I don't know anything.'

'So what should I do? I do love her, you know. More than anything. She is The One and she always has been, but now she hates me for not understanding what she wanted. But how was I to know? How is any bloke to know what women want? And now I've lost her.'

'Maybe not—' I started.

'I have. She said it's thanks to you.'

'Thanks to me? No, Sam. All I have tried to do is go along with the plan.'

'But you never really liked me. did you? Did you say something to turn her against me?'

'I . . . Um. No. Not really.' But too late – he'd heard the hesitation in my voice. 'OK. I might have said something about you not listening to what she wanted.'

'But she never said. I thought she was OK with the list.'

'I think she wanted to make you happy. Listen. Let me try and persuade her to talk to you. Hold on.'

I put the phone down and raced along the hall to where Marcie was.

'Sam on the phone,' I said urgently. 'Will you talk to him? He sounds ever so sorry.'

Marcie shook her head. 'Too late,' she said.

I went back to the phone. 'Sam, you there? She won't come—'

I was about to say that I would keep trying but he'd hung up.

I put down the phone and burst into tears. *Now everyone is unhappy*, I thought. *I hate weddings.* Suddenly I knew exactly where I wanted to go. I wanted to go upstairs to my bed, get under the duvet with Sergeant Ted and never come out again.

Chapter Twelve

Meeting the Planets

'So what are you going to do?' asked Demi when I met up with her and Maryam at lunch break on Monday.

'I've decided, I'm going to go into Osbury after school. I'm going to find Nessa and give her back the Zodiac phone and tell her that I don't want to be a Zodiac Girl or have anything to do with it any more.'

'But why?' asked Maryam. 'It's not her fault.'

'Yes it is. Sam thinks that it's my fault that Marcie called the wedding off, that I talked her out of it, but I didn't, not really. OK, I may have said a few things but I never thought this would happen. The last few weeks have been the weirdest of my life, and ever since I won that stupid Zodiac thing and Nessa started giving me advice, everything has gone wrong. All that stuff about not resisting. Maybe if I give the prize back, that will fix it. Tell them to let some other girl be the Zodiac Girl.'

'I'll do it! If I didn't have choir rehearsal tonight, I'd come with you and tell them myself,' said Maryam.

'I'd love to be a Zodiac girl and have someone like Nessa give me advice.'

'And me,' said Demi. 'If I didn't have orchestra after school, I'd say I'd be the Zodiac Girl. I reckoned it looked fun and there are two weeks left. Who knows what could happen? And Uri said that there could only be one girl chosen at a time. One girl, one month. Remember? So yeah, maybe if you back out, one of us can be it – I bet there are loads more wedding goodies to try out.'

Hearing Demi and Maryam enthuse about being a Zodiac Girl threw me and made me wonder if I'd made the wrong decision. Maybe it wasn't Nessa's fault. *Oh no*, I thought, *here I go again! Can't make a decision and stick to it.*

'Well, for me it's been a curse, not a blessing,' I said as the bell rang and we gathered our things up to go into afternoon class. *Or has it been a blessing?* I asked myself as we made our way to the science labs. *Yes, being blamed for breaking up Marcie's engagement was bad but trying out the list of wedding options has been fun in the end. It has. Shall I give Nessa another chance? See what else she has in store? Oh God, another decision.* 'I think I am going mad,' I said.

'*Going* mad? You always were,' teased Demi.

'No, really. I *hate* being a Libran. It's supposed to be a nice sign, easy-going, balanced, but I think it's the *worst* sign of the whole Zodiac, like – being able to see both sides, it means that it's hard to make a decision about anything, I'm always so busy weighing up and making sure that what I decide is balanced.'

'You can't change your birth sign though,' said Maryam. 'It's not like changing your name.'

'I know, so that's it then. I am doomed for life, cursed for eternity, I will forever not be able to make up my mind about anything and so will have to suffer the consequences. God, now I'm depressed as well as going mad.'

'So make a few decisions,' said Maryam. 'Defy the traits of your birth sign and make a few choices. In fact, we are going to have to do that at the beginning of next week anyway. Remember, our subjects for next year?'

'Oh that. Arghhhhhh! I'd forgotten about all that over the weekend. What with Marcie blubbing all over the place and everyone blaming me and Sam mad with me and being in the doghouse, I'd totally forgotten about deciding what stupid course I want to take.'

Demi squeezed my arm. 'So now you're going mad, and you're depressed and stressed too,' she said.

I nodded. 'And it's only Monday! So, OK, I am going to make a choice and this is it. I am going to go to Osbury, talk to Nessa and ask just what this whole Zodiac thing is all about. She said she was my guardian and here to help, so get me out of this mess, Nessa – let's see if you can!'

Demi glanced at Maryam. 'I suppose it's a start,' she said.

Maryam took my other arm. 'And we love you whatever you decide or don't. To us, you're just Chloe, our lovely mate who can never make up her mind.'

After school, I caught the bus as usual but instead of getting off at my stop to go home, I stayed on the bus until it got to Osbury. I'd texted Nessa in the afternoon break and said I'd like to come and see her and she texted back that she'd be in the Europa cafe and that it was perfect timing for me to meet up with her and the others. *Yeah, right,* I'd thought.

Once off the bus, I made my way over the green where the wedding show had been held and saw Europa in front of me. It looked warm and cosy inside and I was looking forward to one of the fantastic hot chocolate drinks that Joe, who runs the place, makes. Inside, the cafe was empty apart from Joe who was busy behind his counter. He looked up and smiled when he saw me. 'Ah, Zodiac Girl,' he said. 'Welcome.'

'Quiet night,' I replied. 'Where is everybody?'

'Here in a moment,' he said. 'Nessa said you

wanted to talk. Until then, sit, sit, and I'll bring you your special.'

I did as I was told and soon after, he brought me a cup of steaming hot chocolate. 'Hmm, delicious,' I said as I took the first sip. It really was like nothing I had ever tasted before, with just the perfect balance of chocolate and creaminess. Soon after, Nessa and Uri arrived, followed by PJ and Hermie. They gave me a wave then went to get their drinks. *One, two, three, four, five. Five of the planet wedding company*, I thought. *I wonder where the other five are.*

Hermie, who was looking as handsome as ever, moved a couple of tables together and beckoned me over to sit with them.

'So, Chloe,' said Nessa once everyone was settled. 'You wanted our advice.'

'Yes. I mean no. I mean—'

All five of them burst out laughing.

'Why are you laughing?' I asked.

'Because that's so typically Libran – yes, no, can't make up your mind,' Nessa replied.

'Tell me about it. It's been a nightmare lately. I feel like I've been going mad.'

The five nodded solemnly and I felt like they understood.

'What exactly is the problem?' asked Hermie.

'Oh, just everything,' I began and before I knew it,

I was telling the whole story from the very beginning, from when I started the Bridesmaids' Club to last weekend when Sam appeared as unhappy as Marcie and thinking that maybe I turned her against him. They didn't interrupt or make faces like they were judging me, they just listened. 'So that's it, really,' I said when I had finished.

'Hmm, a right mess,' said Joe.

'You can say that again,' I said.

'Hmm, a right mess,' Joe repeated, then grinned.

'But what about you, Chloe?' asked Nessa. 'I see you've 'ad a difficult angle with Mars in your 'oroscope. Is there something else that you're not tellin' us about?'

'Er . . . yes . . . no, um, Mars. That's listed as Mario on the phone, isn't it? So why haven't I met him then?'

'Oh, you will,' Nessa replied. 'Soon in fact. 'E deals with goals and ambitions. That's 'is area. Ring a bell?'

'Sort of. School. Everyone's on about what we're going to be when we leave, like what job do we want to do, so yes, that's been hard too. Goals and ambitions. See, I haven't a clue.'

The five of them laughed again.

'Why do you keep laughing?' I asked. 'It's so *not* funny. In fact these past weeks have been the hardest in my life. I just don't get this whole Zodiac Girl thing.'

'Some Zodiac Girls get who we really are,' said Hermie.

'And ozzers don't. They rationalize vot happens to zem to fitting zeir understandings of zeir world,' said PJ.

'Like Chloe,' said Nessa. 'Doesn't matter though, does it?'

'Maybe it does,' said PJ.

Make up your minds, I thought as I tried to make sense of what they were trying to tell me. Whatever one said, a moment later another contradicted it. For a second I wondered if they were making fun of me by mimicking my trouble making up my mind.

'Are you making fun of me?' I asked.

Uri grinned. 'Maybe, maybe not.'

'There *are* two sides to every situation,' added Nessa. 'Nothin' wrong with that.'

'Unless it messes your head up,' said Hermie, jutting his chin in my direction.

'Exactly,' I said. 'It can *really* mess your head up and has done mine. I don't know what to think or do for the best any more and that's why I needed to see you. I need your help.'

'What can we do?' asked Nessa. 'We've been through your wedding options.'

'I need to get Marcie and Sam back together. OK, she was freaked by his mad wedding list but I think that she genuinely does love him. She's been so miserable since they broke up and he sounded really upset too.'

'Ah,' said Nessa. 'True love. Now that I do know about.'

'Marcie said that *I* had shown her about love, and in doing that I had made her see that Sam wasn't there for her,' I explained. 'I didn't mean to do that.'

'Ah,' said Joe. 'But a break might be good for them. Absence makes ze heart grow fonder.'

'No, sometimes absence makes the heart grow cold and forget,' said Uri.

'So what is love then?' I asked. 'How do you know when it's true?'

'You feel beautiful and everythin' feels 'armonious,' said Nessa.

'No,' said PJ. 'Eet can also be ze pain, passion, torment, a sweet agony but you can't escape, like an addiction.'

'No. It's when you feel your very best with someone and they feel their very best with you,' said Nessa.

'No,' said Uri. 'It's when you can be your worst with someone and they still love you, like first thing in the morning when you haven't even combed your hair or when you're having a lousy day and don't feel like seeing anyone.'

'No,' said Joe. 'It's more simple than that. Love is

unconditional. You will do and go anywhere for someone without expectations. The minute there are
expectations, then it's not true love, it's selfish love.'

'But people are only human,' said Nessa.

'But love is divine,' said Hermie. 'I think true love is
when you and your lover are in true communication,
like you know what each other thinks and feels.'

'No,' said PJ. 'It's a journey, a learning process.'

They're making fun again, and talk about confusing! I
thought as I watched them put forward different argu-
ments and angles and points of view. It was like
watching a ball at a tennis match. One side and then
the other, back again, then back again, and everything
everybody said seemed to be right. Actually, it was like
living inside my head, always seeing one side and then
the other. These planet wedding people weren't being
any help at all. They were as confused as I was and
couldn't agree on anything.

'I don't think you know any more than I do,' I said.

Nessa smiled. 'Yes and no. We were demonstratin''
that it's true, there are always many sides to every situation and although confusin' sometimes, Chloe, seein''
the various angles is what will give you your strength.'

'Strength to do what?'

'Whatever you decide to do in your future,' said
Uri.

'My future. What about now? What about Sam? How can I help him to get Marcie back?'

'Hmm. First Sam has to let Marcie go,' said Uri. 'If love is true, if you let it go and it keeps coming back, then it is meant to be.'

PJ scoffed. 'How idealistic is zat? No. You have to vork at it to make love happen. Tell her how he is feelings, voo her to vin her heart again.'

''E shouldn't be too intense though, or desperate,' said Nessa 'Tell Sam to pursue 'er with beautiful things, flowers, perfume, chocolates.'

'Or maybe she should forget him and move on,' said Uri.

This time I laughed. 'You lot can't make your mind up about anything! You really are worse than me. All you do is contradict each other. You know what? *I* am going to decide.'

They all nodded like children who had been reprimanded.

'Good,' said Nessa. 'What are you going to do?'

'Romance,' I said. 'That's something us Librans know about. I am going to call Sam and tell him that in order to win Marcie back, he needs to romance her back. I like your plan, Nessa. A lovely evening. Flowers. Maybe a restaurant with gypsy music. Champagne. Moonlight.'

Nessa was watching me with a proud expression. 'Exactly,' she said.

But then another thought occurred to me. 'Or do you think the saying 'Treat them mean to keep them keen' is true? He shouldn't call her and then she'll miss him and think about him. Sometimes people want what they can't have.'

PJ nodded. 'Zat iz true. Ze lure of ze unattainable.'

'No,' said Nessa. 'Maybe in the beginnin', but these two are far down the line. They were engaged, for goodness sake. Way past the time of playin' games. No, Chloe, you tell Sam that if 'e doesn't want to lose Marcie, 'e has to swallow 'is pride, buy the most beautiful bunch of flowers 'e can find, and keep pursuin' 'er like 'e's 'er slave until she gives in.'

'I agree,' I said. 'He must romance her.'

'So what are you waitin' for?' asked Nessa with a smile.

Joe got up and got a piece of paper and six pens. 'For ze plan,' he said.

'Excellent,' I said as I took a pen and wrote the word 'Romance' at the top of the paper.

Chapter Thirteen

Goals, Schmoals

Tuesday went by. Wednesday. Thursday. I hadn't heard from Marcie, I hadn't heard from Sam, I hadn't heard from Mario, the Mars person, even though Nessa said that I had an encounter coming up with him. I knew I didn't have much time left and that I had to have decided my subjects by the end of the week. I had been up late every night trying to decide, talking it over with Mum and even with Jane and Clare. They all offered what advice they could and depending on who I last talked to, my career choice kept changing. Fashion, lawyer, vet, art, science, languages – I still couldn't decide. It felt hopeless. I just couldn't make up my mind.

And then on Friday, in school assembly, Mr Fitzpatrick, our headmaster, announced at assembly, 'We have a very special guest visiting the school today. Mario Ares, teacher of martial arts, ex-soldier and expert careers advisor. If you're in any doubt what your goals are, this is the man to talk to.'

Tadah! I thought. *He's my man.*

I signed up immediately and got an appointment for lunch time. My session was to take place in the library, so as soon as the bell went I made my way down there. I knew it was him as soon as I walked in. A tall handsome black man sitting behind the desk, he had the same charisma as the other people in the planet business, larger than life. He smiled when he saw me, revealing a perfect set of Hollywood white teeth. *Nessa and her pals must have the same dentist because they all have perfect teeth,* I thought as I approached him. I felt a rush of adrenalin, like I was about to meet a famous person.

'So, Zodiac Girl,' he said when I took the seat that he indicated in front of me. 'Third week in. How's it going?'

'OK, I guess. Nessa said I only get to be Zodiac Girl for four weeks.'

'One month, one girl,' said Mario, repeating the words that Uri had said. 'I trust you have been making the most of it.'

'Yes . . . um, maybe, but what exactly does it mean?'

'Didn't Nessa or one of the others explain?'

'Sort of. She said that for one month, I got the guidance of her as my guardian plus the other planets that were prominent in my chart. At first I thought it was just to do with business. Like the ones I met all seem to be in the wedding market. But why the planet theme?

I'm beginning to get the feeling that there's more to it. And you're not to do with weddings and you know about the Zodiac thing, so who exactly are you?'

Mario considered me for a moment like he was weighing up who I was and whether I had a brain or not.

'My connection with weddings is that I work with brides and grooms wanting to tone up and get fit for the day,' Mario replied. 'You know, as a personal trainer. I set the goals, I put them through their paces. I get results. I get them looking their very best physically. That's my involvement. But there's more to it than that, and I think deep down, you know that.'

I thought about all the times that Nessa and the others had seemed to know exactly when I needed them, about how weird it was that they just happened to offer all of the weddings on the list, and how everything about them felt a bit magical. Maybe I would never totally understand what being a Zodiac Girl was all about but for the moment I was happy just to let them help me, so I decided not to ask any more questions. 'Yes, I think I do!'

Mario looked at me as if he was trying to gauge me and I looked back at him with the same expression.

'So, Miss Zodiac. Career choices. Subject choices for your GCSEs?' he finally asked.

'Haven't a clue. At least, I had ideas but I keep

changing my mind. That's because I am a Libran – see, I don't know much about astrology, Mr Ares, but I do know that Librans are represented by the symbol of the scales – that's because they like to weigh and balance all sides of an argument before they make up their mind. I used to think it was a weakness but now Nessa has helped me to understand that actually it's a strength.'

Mario looked amused. 'Is that so?'

'Why are you laughing? Why do all of you in the planet business laugh at me?'

'Not laughing at,' said Mario, 'laughing with. It's a joy to have astrology explained to me . . . And so articulately.'

'Well, I don't know how much you know about it,' I said. 'I don't assume that everyone knows as much about it as I do now. Uri and Nessa explained a bit about it ever since I became Zodiac Girl.'

'They are to be commended,' said Mario.

'Anyway, with the gift of seeing all sides of an argument,' I continued, 'I could be a lawyer or a counsellor but then, on the other hand, Librans have a good sense of beauty and harmony so I could do art or design or something. I'm still not sure though.'

'Follow your gut, then go for it,' said Mario. 'From all I have heard, I would have thought that your perfect job was staring you in the face.'

'My face? My perfect job? No. What?'

'Sometimes people miss what is right in front of them. I can't tell you though. It has to come from you.'

'Give me a clue,' I said.

'It's a natural talent. It's something you love.'

I sat and thought. And thought. And thought. Fashion. Art. Animals. All options I had considered before casting them aside.

'Cast your mind back,' said Mario. 'Back over the years.'

Home. Parents. Mum and Dad splitting up. Jane. Clare. Marcie. The Bridesmaids' Club. That was my best memory – getting that started, collecting all my data, going to the wedding shows, planning weddings with Demi and Maryam. What else? No. Not what else, that was it! The *Bridesmaids'* Club!

'The Bridesmaids' Club. Of course! But could I? Would I be allowed to? It wouldn't be like a job. It would be like all my dreams come true.'

'Best sort of job, I'd say,' said Mario.

It was like a light had come on in my head. Ping! Obvious. *So* obvious what I should do. I got up and hugged him.

It was perfect, *better* than perfect, and I'd been preparing for it all my life. Wedding planner. *Wedding* planner. That's what I'd do.

Hallelujah! I thought. I couldn't wait to tell Demi

and Maryam. We could start an agency. A photographer and a designer, just what was needed. It needn't be *my* agency, it could be *our* agency. We could be a team. Nessa had said that what I had learned in the last few weeks would last me a lifetime and it was suddenly all fitting into place, like pieces of a jigsaw. Marcie's wedding, not mine. People's weddings, not mine. I had learned that there were many ways of doing things, many sides to an argument, and that was OK. I wouldn't press my clients into *my* perfect wedding, instead I would help them to create *their* perfect day. Yay! I had never felt so happy.

'Thank you, Mr Ares. You really are the best career guide I have ever met,' I said.

Mr Ares smiled. 'You're welcome, although I wouldn't say that I did very much.'

'You pointed me in the right direction and that's what I'll do too when I work as a wedding planner. I won't impose my ideas, I'll point people in the direction of what's best for them.'

'Sounds good to me,' said Mr Ares as I headed for the door. Now all that was needed was for Sam to win back Marcie and I could get back to planning my first job – their wedding.

Chapter Fourteen

For Sam

'I know what I want to be,' I said to Demi and Maryam, who were waiting for me outside the library.

Demi rolled her eyes. 'OK. So what's this week's career choice?'

'No. This is it. Really it. I feel so happy, I can't tell you,' I said. 'Least I *can* tell you, finally, I have decided.' I did a little skip and a jump, I felt so good about it.

'OK, so what is it?' asked Maryam.

'Wedding planner.'

'Wedding planner?' they chorused and their faces broke into grins. 'Wedding planner! Of *course*!'

'Totally utterly brilliant,' said Demi.

'Why didn't we think of it?' said Maryam. 'It was staring us in the face.'

'I know,' I said. 'That's what Mario said too.'

'No doubts, no changing your mind?' asked Demi.

I shook my head. 'Nope. I am one hundred per cent

up for this and I think it should herald the end of the Bridesmaids' Club—'

Demi and Maryam's faces dropped. 'No,' gasped Demi. 'But—'

'The end of the Bridesmaids' Club and the *beginning* of the Wedding Planners' team,' I said. 'We run our own agency. You. Me. Weddings R Us. We do the whole thing . . . Outfits, shoes, locations, photos. Honeymoons, themed ceremonies. Whatever you want. Emphasis being on whatever *you* want, and we're talking Velcro, bungee, Bridezilla, etc., etc., here. We will offer traditional and alternative.'

Maryam clapped her hands. 'Yay!' she said.

We put our hands on each other's shoulders and did a skip round.

'And why stop at weddings?' I said after we'd let go. 'If these last weeks have taught me anything, it's to expect the unexpected, right? To be flexible or else you feel let down. Know what I mean?'

'Yeah,' said Demi. 'I guess. So?'

'So. I think we should think bigger than just wedding planners. Why stop at weddings? That week with Marcie's mad list really did teach me to push the boundaries. We could plan all sorts of events. Parties . . . You name it! We could do anything because there's one thing we're good at and that's planning.'

'And research,' Demi added.

'We could maybe even get into TV production and films,' said Maryam.

'We could. OK. So we start with our wedding and party agency and see where we go,' I said. 'We plan, but like we did with Marcie, we go with the flow too.'

I felt ecstatic. My future career was sorted and I'd be doing something that I loved. Thanks to Marcie and Sam and their mad wedding list, it couldn't have turned out better.

'In the meantime, we have our first job,' I said.

'Ah, yes,' said Maryam.

'I think I know,' agreed Demi.

I nodded. 'Sam and Marcie. But our job isn't to plan their wedding. Our job is to get them back together.'

We spent the next few days doing what we did best, and as it was my last week as Zodiac Girl, I decided to make the most of it and ask for Nessa and her friends' help. Together we sourced the best fresh flowers flown in the same morning from Holland. Joe Jupiter let me have his source for the most scrummy soft centre chocolates from Belgium and also gave us a list of the most romantic locations for a cosy candlelit supper. We researched the best music to play to tug at the heartstrings. We found candles that smelt of tuberose and aftershave for Sam to wear, guaranteed to melt the last of Marcie's resistance.

Hermie found me a limo company perfect to take Marcie to the chosen restaurant and I instructed the chauffeur to treat her like a princess.

Uri sourced fun gifts like fluffy teddy bears, balloons that said I Love You, T-shirts that had I'm Sorry written on the front. Hermie found a website that helped write poems in any style – funny, passionate, apologetic. By the time we had finished, not even a person with a heart of stone would be able to turn Sam down.

I made a list of 'ways to win your girlfriend back' and we went round to Sam's house early on Thursday evening. He opened the door looking pale and stressed, just like Marcie had done when she had been over last night.

'And you really think this might work?' he asked, after he let us into his hall and we stepped over roller blades and manoeuvred our way past his bicycle. I handed him the list, which he glanced over.

'All you can do is try,' I said.

'Love favours the brave,' said Demi.

'Love never gives up,' said Maryam.

'Love conquers all,' I said.

Sam smiled. 'What are you three? Love experts?'

'We are. We will be. We're going to be wedding and party planners,' I explained.

Sam laughed. 'Watch out, world.'

'Exactly,' I said.

'So, the list. Do I do it all at once or one at a time?' he asked, sounding nervous, but I was glad to see that he was taking it seriously.

'One at a time at first,' I said, 'and then maybe go for a crescendo-type finale in the restaurant with the violins and candles.'

'You could even sing,' Demi suggested.

'Right,' he said. 'Um. Think I'll start with the chocs.'

'Fingers crossed,' I said.

'And toes.'

He looked so worried and like a little boy that my heart went out to him. With his mop of blond hair and sky-blue eyes, I could see exactly why Marcie had fallen for him. *He's like the Belgian chocolates we were recommending*, I thought, *soft-centred*. I smiled to myself. *This is all good training. I bet loads of couples almost break up pre-wedding. Getting people to make up is going to be part of the job.*

'Funny isn't it, Sam?' I said. 'I did your list and now you're doing mine.'

He nodded. 'I think yours might be more the thing,' he said. 'I never was very good at romance and girlie stuff. See, I grew up with two older brothers. How was I supposed to learn? My defence was to pretend I didn't care, to make fun of it like I did about your Bridesmaids' Club. I am sorry, Chloe. See, that club represented everything I didn't know about and . . . if I'm honest, I was threatened by it.'

'Really?' I asked. I was surprised. Sam had always seemed so confident. Maybe there were two sides to him as well as everything else! I gave him a massive hug to show all was forgiven.

'Aah!' cooed Demi and Maryam, who were looking on.

I pulled away from the hug. 'So now it's over to you, Sam,' I said. 'Romance and a grand gesture, that's what's called for. Something to knock her off her feet. And have no fear, I think you will succeed because Marcie does love you and love always wins in the end.'

Sam grinned from ear to ear. 'And she loves you too. Room for both of us?'

'Deffo,' I said again. 'And oh, I just remembered! You're compatible astrologically. I forgot to mention that. A friend of mine told me at the wedding show. Marcie's Leo and you're Sagittarius, both fire signs. A great match so you're bound to get on.'

'Wow! Is there anything you don't know about when it comes to romance?' asked Sam.

'Probably, but I am going to make it my business to find out.'

Sam grinned, then saluted. 'Right, Captain Chloe. Love Cadet Sam, reporting for duty.'

The three of us saluted him back. 'Mission Get Back Marcie. Proceed.'

Epilogue

The Hendy wedding got a double-page spread in the local paper, the *Osbury Times*, with eight fabulous photos. It read:

Marcie Bradbury and Sam Hendy were married on Sunday afternoon at a private chapel in Osbury. The bride, Marcie, and bridesmaids, Chloe, Demi and Maryam, were beautiful in ivory silk designed by up-and-coming designer Nessa of Celestial Creations. All the girls carried bouquets of cream roses and ivy. The groom was breathtakingly handsome in a white suit.

The reception was held at Osbury Hall Hotel, where the guests feasted on a gourmet meal provided by Joe Jupiter of Europa Catering. As the guests were eating, the groom disappeared, later to be seen flying overhead in a small aircraft that looped the loop and wrote the words 'Marcie, I love you' in the sky. Moments later, he was joined by several other small aircraft flown by members of the Celestial Wedding Company, and between them thousands of white rose petals were showered down upon the wedding party, causing the whole area to smell like a rose garden after the rain. The bride is said to have been 'knocked off her feet by the gesture'. Later, she praised her husband and her bridesmaids, saying that they had organized every last detail and made her day everything she had ever hoped for.

After the reception, the party retired to the gardens, where a variety of activities had been organized. Guests tried roller-skating, trampolining, some even dressed up in fancy dress, and it was hilarious to see Spiderman sipping champagne with a gorilla and Superwoman enjoying canapés with a Viking warrior. Towards the end of the afternoon, the groom had a go at bungee jumping from a large crane that had been erected around the back of the hotel. As he leaped into the air, a banner unfolded behind him, saying 'Marcie, I've really fallen for you'.

Everyone agreed that it was the most romantic and the most fun wedding they had ever attended. Sadly, the groom had to be taken to the hospital soon after his jump. He was suffering with whiplash to his neck but is said to be recovering nicely.

Are you a typical Libra?

You go out shopping for a new party dress and you find two you really like. What do you do?
A) Flip a coin – you will never be able to choose.
B) Ask your friend her advice and choose her favourite.
C) Buy both. You'll need another one eventually!

A new girl joins your school and she is wearing shoes that are really unfashionable right now. What do you do?
A) Shrug it off and go and introduce yourself. Maybe they're so ugly they're actually cool!
B) Vow not to be friends with her. There's no excuse for bad shoes.
C) Go and tell her that nobody likes her shoes. Somebody needs to tell her!

You go to the cinema with a group of friends, but none of you can decide what to see. What type of film would you most enjoy?
A) Horror – something with lots of gruesome monsters to scare you all!
B) Romantic comedy – something to make you laugh

C) Weepy romance – a film where you can gush over the gorgeous lead and have a good cry!

Your parents ask what you would like for your birthday but you aren't exactly sure what you want. What do you say?

A) You don't mind. Maybe something to help you with your schoolwork or maybe a new pair of earrings or maybe a CD or maybe . . .

B) Some money so you can go out and buy some beautiful new clothes.

C) Don't be silly you know exactly what you want – that stunning diamond necklace you saw when you were out shopping last week.

A friend calls you while you are doing chores for your mum, to ask if you want to come and join a group of them who are on their way to the park. You say no as you still have a lot to do but she keeps on asking as she really wants you to go. What do you do?

A) Say sorry but you have to do your chores or you will get into trouble when your mum comes home, but maybe another time.

B) Decide to rush through your chores in half an hour and then join them.

C) Go straight away and leave your chores for another day. Mum won't be too cross!

It's your sister's birthday in a week and she really wants a CD that costs £10, which is just the amount you have to spend, but you really want to buy a new top as well. What do you do?

A) Buy your sister the CD she wants – it's what good sisters do!

B) Buy your sister a CD that costs only £5 and spend the rest on your new top.

C) Buy yourself a new top costing £10 and tell your sister they didn't have the CD so you will look again next time!

How did you score?

Mostly As – a little bit Libra

Hmm, it sounds like your inner Libra is a bit too hidden. Embrace your indecisiveness!

Mostly Bs – lots of Libra

You know your Libra limitations and you embrace your Libra loveliness – go you!

Mostly Cs – LOADS of Libra

How do you ever get anything done? Seeing both sides of the story is great, but you have to make up your mind eventually!